THE USBORNE BOOK OF

PAPER ENGINEERING

Fiona Watt

Designed by Vicki Groombridge
Paper engineering consultant: Iain Ashman
Illustrated by John Woodcock • Photographs by Howard Allman
Models made by Tamsin Howe, Jan McCafferty and Zoe Wray
Series editor: Cheryl Evans

Contents

Before you begin

Paper engineering is making cards and models which have parts that pop out, turn, move up and down or from side to side. Before you begin any of the projects in this book, read through these two pages as they give you lots of hints and tips for making all the cards and models.

Templates

For most of the projects you will need to trace at least one template, like the one below. The steps on the right show you an easy way of using carbon paper to transfer a template onto the paper you are using to make a card or model.

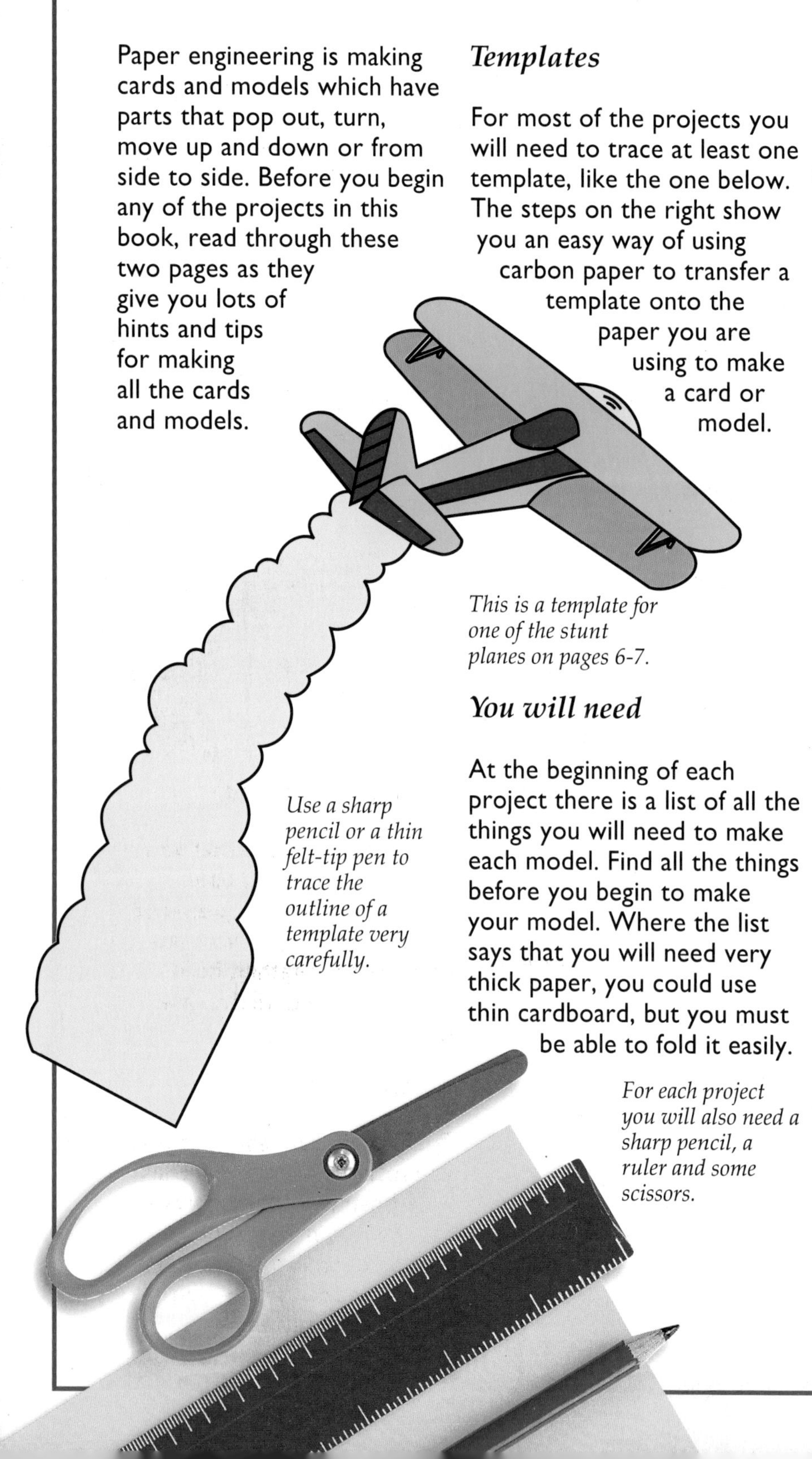

This is a template for one of the stunt planes on pages 6-7.

Use a sharp pencil or a thin felt-tip pen to trace the outline of a template very carefully.

You will need

At the beginning of each project there is a list of all the things you will need to make each model. Find all the things before you begin to make your model. Where the list says that you will need very thick paper, you could use thin cardboard, but you must be able to fold it easily.

For each project you will also need a sharp pencil, a ruler and some scissors.

Tracing a template

Use a sharp pencil.

1. Lay some tracing paper over the template and secure it with paper clips. Trace the template with a sharp pencil or a thin pen.

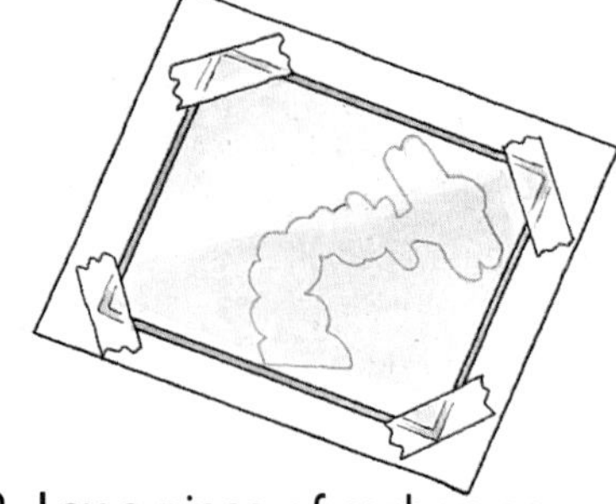

2. Lay a piece of carbon paper over the paper you are using for your model. Lay your tracing on top of it. Secure both pieces of paper with tape.

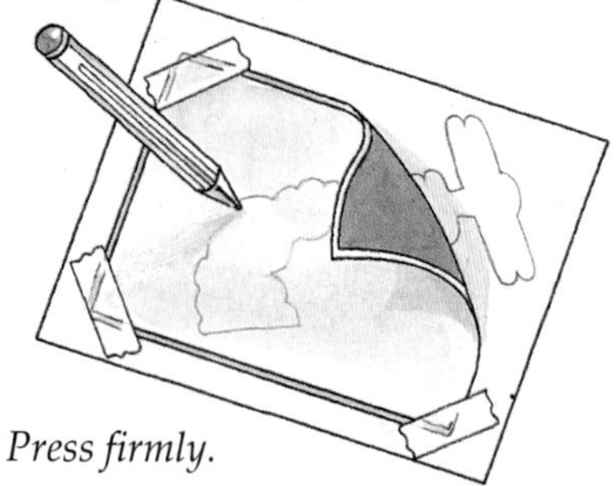

Press firmly.

3. Go over your tracing with a ballpoint pen. Remove the tracing paper and carbon paper. The template will have transferred to your paper.

Shiny paper

Straws

Beads

Bright embroidery thread

Self-adhesive shapes

Sequins

Scoring

It's important that you score a line before you fold it, so that the folded edge will be neat and crisp. The best thing to use for scoring is a ballpoint pen which has run out of ink. If you are scoring a straight line, run the ballpoint pen along the edge of a ruler (see below). In this book, all the lines you need to score are shown on the templates by dotted lines.

Make sure you score all the dotted lines before you glue any part of your model together.

Cutting out

You can use a pair of scissors to cut out all the pieces for most of the projects, but for the best results, use a craft knife. You can buy one from an art or craft store. Be extremely careful when you cut out shapes with it.

This parrot's head is decorated with layers of tissue paper.

Hold the ruler firmly and press hard with the pen to score a straight line on your model.

Folding and gluing

It is very important that you fold all your scored lines before you glue the pieces of your model. When you glue two pieces together, hold them in place until the glue has dried.

Decorating

The photograph above shows you many of the things which have been used to decorate the models in this book. It is best to decorate each piece of your model before you glue them together.

Snapping crocodile

Hidden inside this model is a mechanism which makes the crocodile's mouth snap as you pull and push its tail. The templates are on page 35.

You will need: a piece of thick green paper 42 x 30 cm (17 x 12in); craft knife; scissors; glue; pens, scraps of paper, paint or self-adhesive shapes for decorating.

1. Trace and cut out the templates for the head, body and tail. Trace all the dotted lines and score along them. Decorate each piece.

2. Fold all the scored lines on the tail part. Glue the two thin tabs on the tail and press the sides onto them. Hold them until the glue dries.

Use white paint or typewriter correction fluid to decorate the teeth.

3. Turn the tail over and fold the feet at right angles to the body. Glue the small triangular tab on the side and press the end of the tongue onto it.

4. Fold all the scored lines on the head. Put glue on the two small tabs at the back of the head. Press the part with slots onto the tabs.

Press on self-adhesive shapes after you have made your crocodile, or dip a cork or sponge in paint and dab it all over the pieces before you make it.

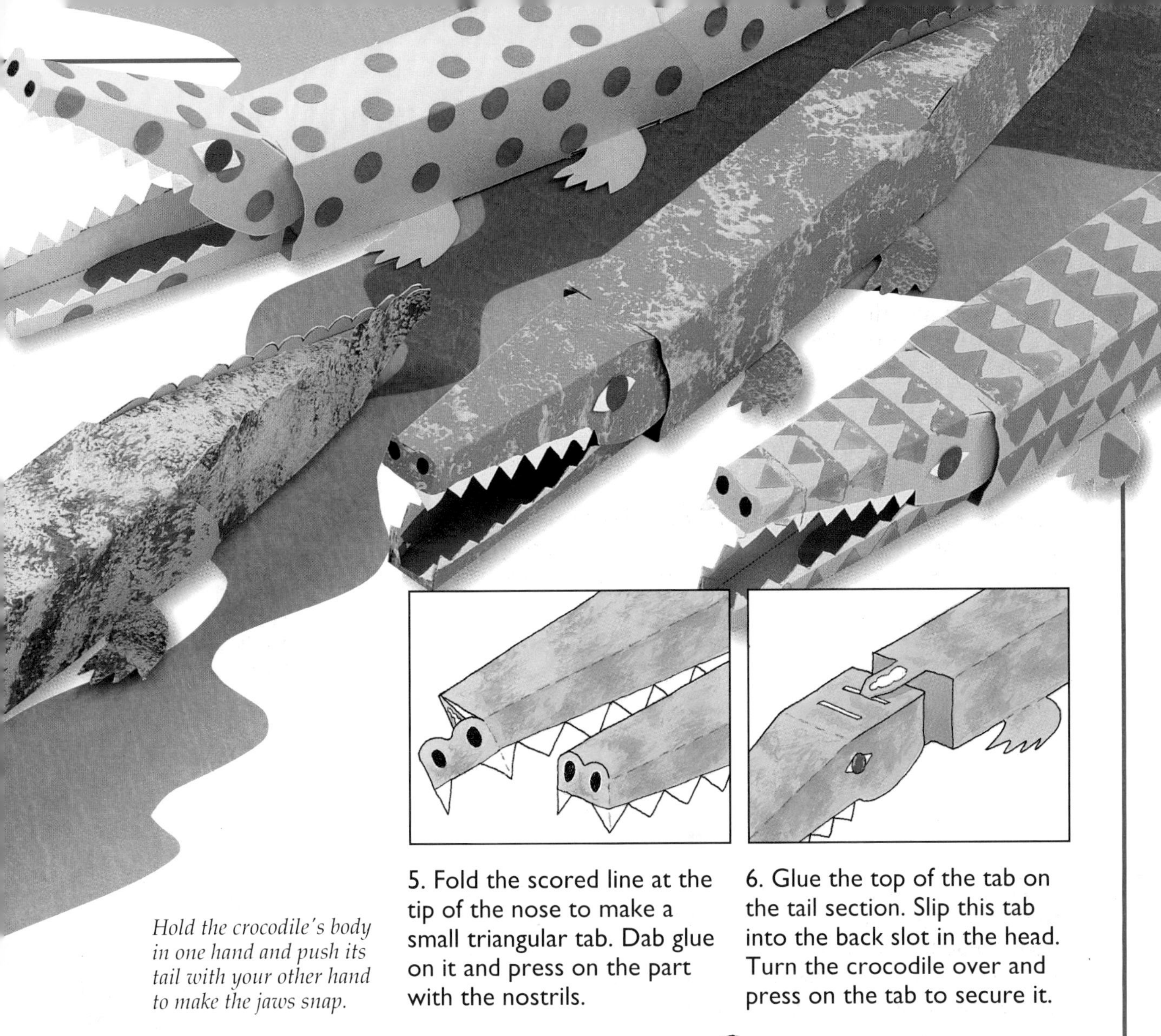

Hold the crocodile's body in one hand and push its tail with your other hand to make the jaws snap.

5. Fold the scored line at the tip of the nose to make a small triangular tab. Dab glue on it and press on the part with the nostrils.

6. Glue the top of the tab on the tail section. Slip this tab into the back slot in the head. Turn the crocodile over and press on the tab to secure it.

7. Fold along all the scored lines on the body part. Glue the tiny tabs at the front of the jaw and press the sides onto them.

8. Put the tail and head inside the body and slip the feet through the slots. Glue the tab on the side of the body and press the top onto it.

9. Push the tail forward as far as you can. Glue the tab and push it into the slot on the head. Put your finger into the mouth and press on the tab.

Stunt plane card

Use this template for the bottom plane on your card. The template for the top plane is on page 2.

Trace the detail from this plane or draw some of your own.

Straight end

These planes use a paper engineering mechanism which allows the planes to shoot up into the air when you open the card.

You will need: two pieces of thick paper 30 x 20cm (12 x 8in); a smaller piece of thick paper for the planes; scraps of bright paper for decorating the backgrounds; tracing paper; felt-tip pens; craft knife; glue.

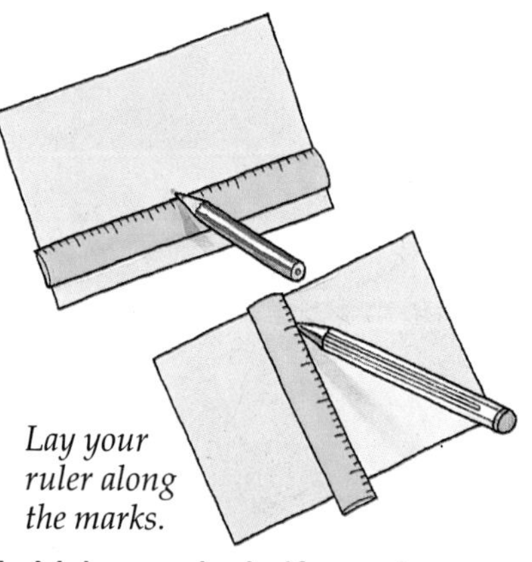

Lay your ruler along the marks.

1. Make marks halfway along (15cm/6in) on both pieces of paper. Score them lightly (see page 3) and fold them in half.

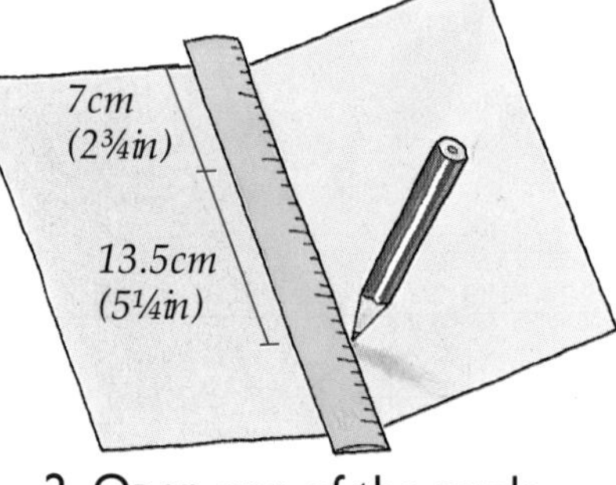

2. Open one of the cards. Mark two dots on the fold 7cm (2¾in) and 13.5cm (5¼in) from the top.

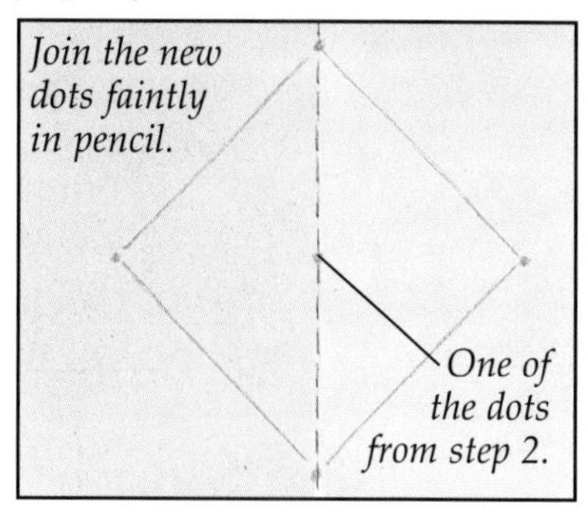

3. Add dots 2cm (¾in) above, below and at either side of each dot from step 2. Join the new dots to make two diamonds.

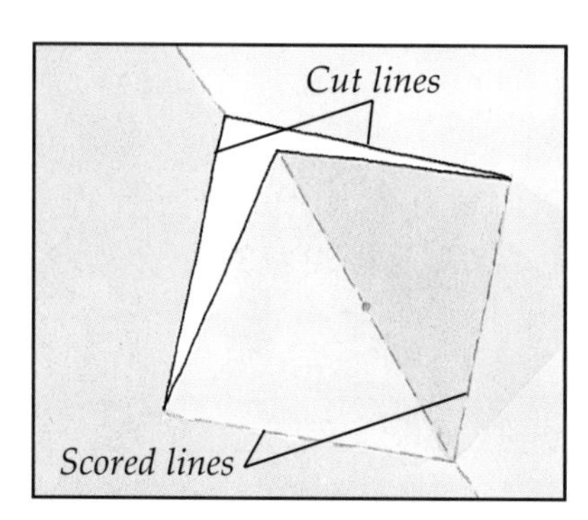

4. Cut along the lines which join the dot at the top with those at the sides. Score along the bottom two lines.

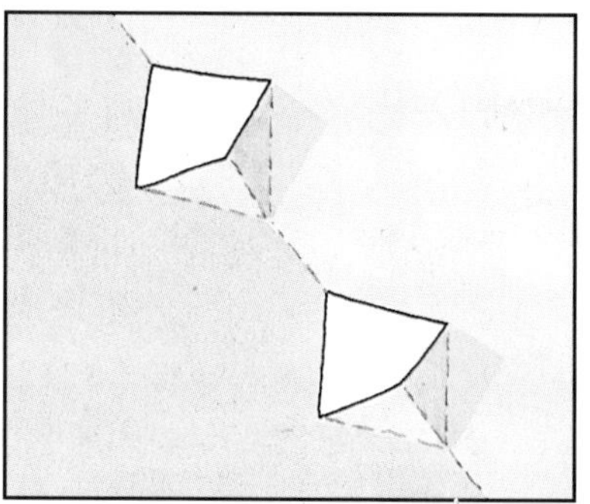

5. Fold each point by pushing the diamond up from below. Fold the front of the card over at the same time.

Decorate your planes before you cut them out.

6. Trace the templates of the planes onto the smaller paper. Use pens to decorate them, then cut them out.

7. Glue the right-hand side of the top diamond. Press on the top plane, lining up its bottom edge with the scored line.

8. Glue the right-hand side of the other diamond. Line up the end of the banner with the middle fold on the diamond.

9. Glue around the edge of the other folded card. Lay the plane card on top, matching the edges. Decorate the card.

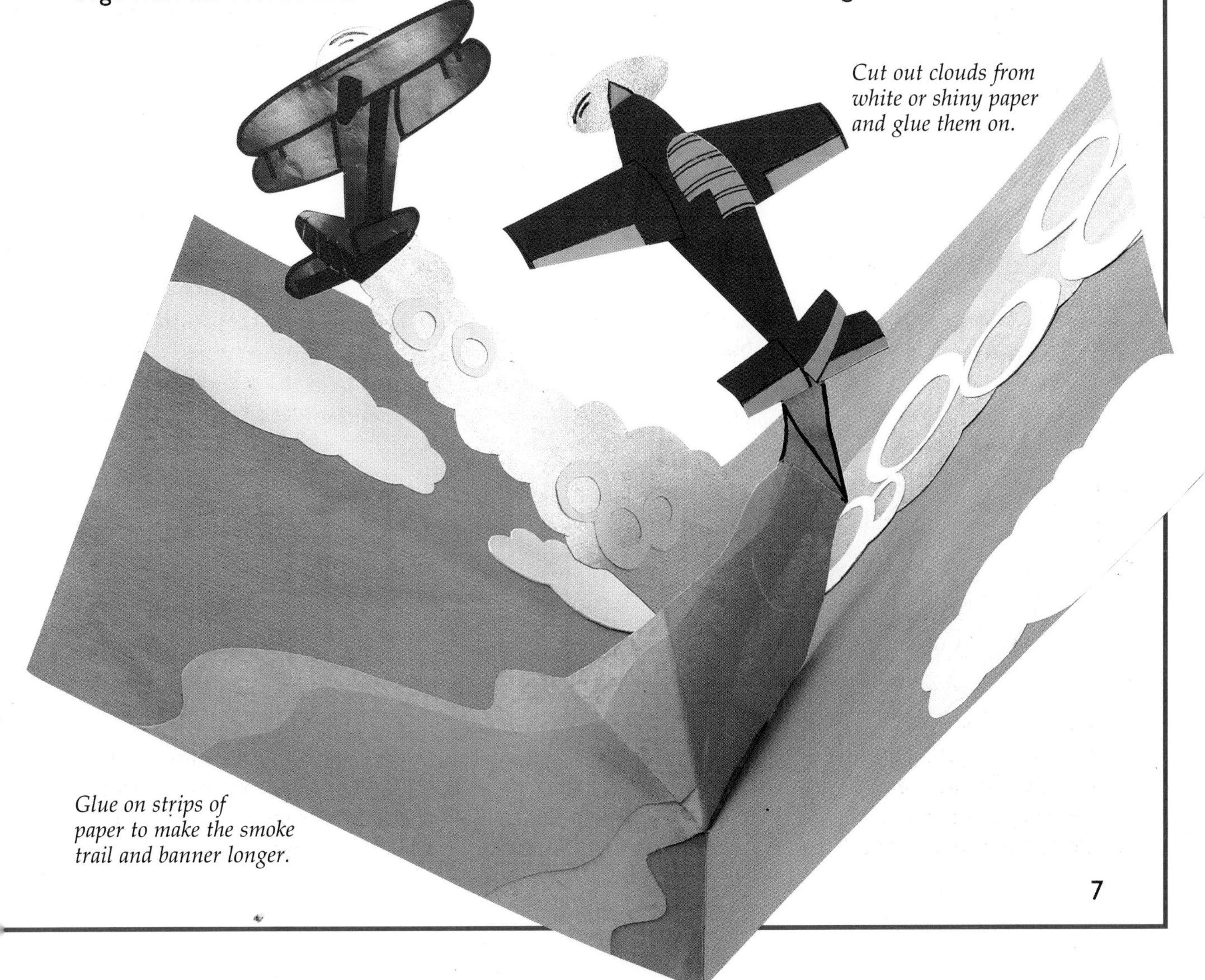

Hungry frog

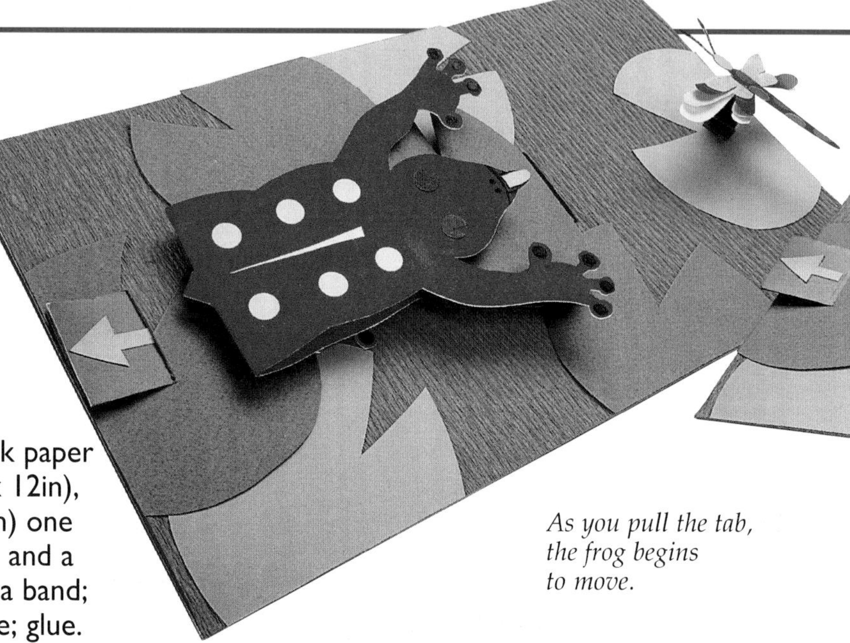
As you pull the tab, the frog begins to move.

When you pull the tab the frog leaps out to try and catch the dragonfly. This is a mechanism which you often find in pop-up books.

You will need: a piece of thick paper for the base 27 x 30cm (10½ x 12in), two pieces 12 x 25cm (5 x 10in) one for the slider and one the frog, and a piece 8 x 2cm (3¼ x ¾in) for a band; paper for decorating; craft knife; glue.

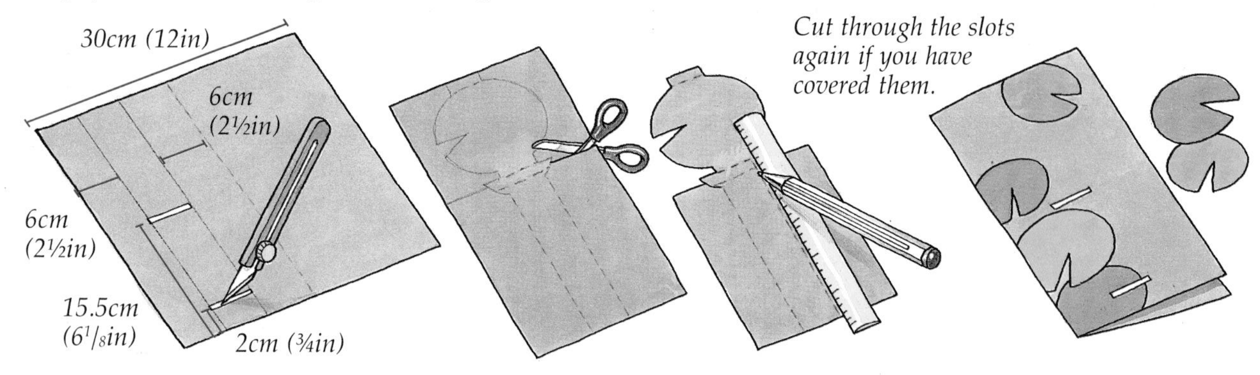

Cut through the slots again if you have covered them.

1. Score a line halfway (15cm/ 6in) along the base. Rule a line 6cm (2¾in) from the edge, and from the scored line. Cut slots between the lines as shown.

2. Trace the lilypad and slider on page 31 onto a middle-sized piece of paper. Cut around the outline then score along all the dotted lines.

3. Trace the lilypad in the bottom corner onto paper several times and cut them out. Fold the base in half then glue the lilypads on the front.

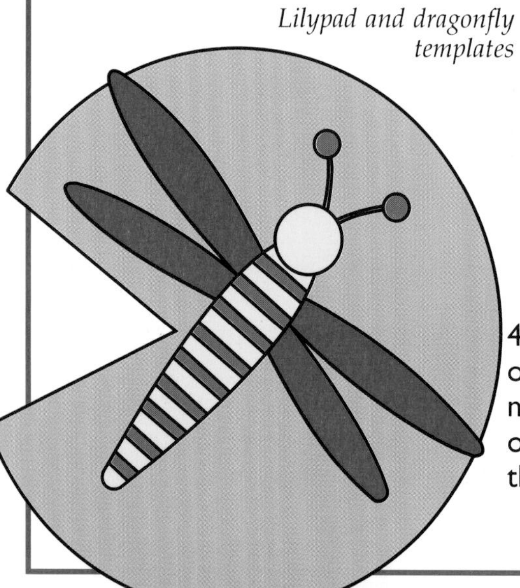
Lilypad and dragonfly templates

Gluing the sides into the middle makes the slider stronger.

4. Fold the long scored lines on the slider. Glue along the middle of the slider and fold one side onto it. Then glue the other side down too.

5. Fold the smallest strip of paper around the slider to make a band. Run it along the slider to make sure that it moves easily, then glue it.

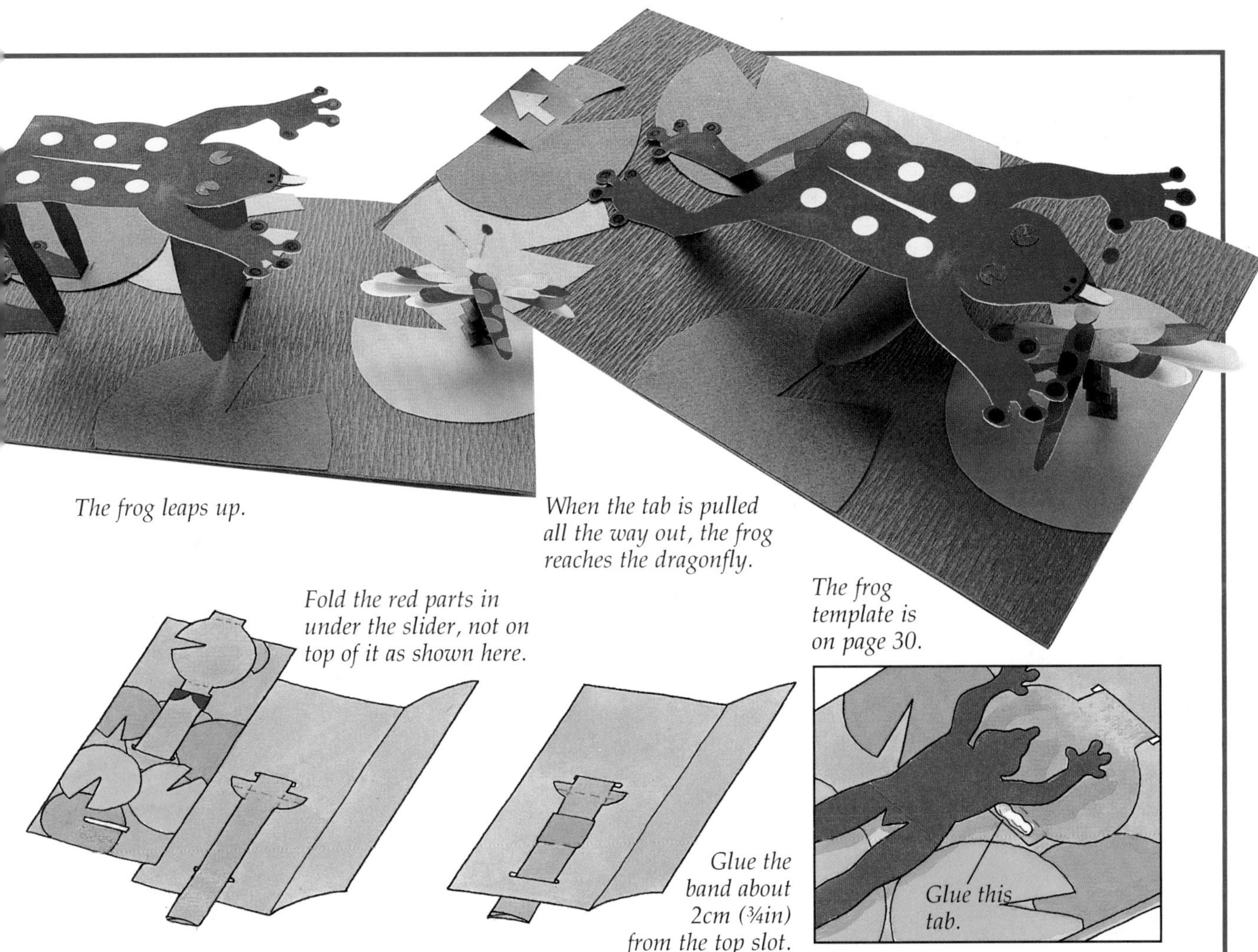

The frog leaps up.

When the tab is pulled all the way out, the frog reaches the dragonfly.

Fold the red parts in under the slider, not on top of it as shown here.

The frog template is on page 30.

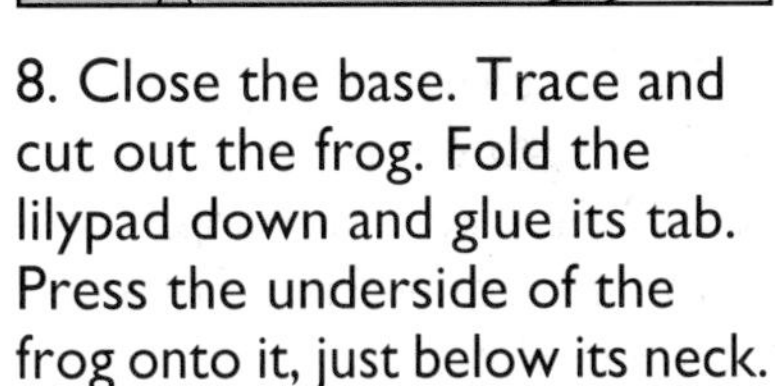

Glue the band about 2cm (¾in) from the top slot.

6. Slide the band off the slider then push it into the top slot. Fold in the parts shown here in red, push them through the slot, then open them out.

7. Slip the band back onto the slider then push the slider out through the bottom slot. Put a drop of glue under the band and press it onto the base.

8. Close the base. Trace and cut out the frog. Fold the lilypad down and glue its tab. Press the underside of the frog onto it, just below its neck.

Pull the tab to make the frog jump.

9. Score the dotted lines on the frog and fold its feet under its body. Put a little glue under its feet and press the frog flat onto the card.

10. Trace and cut out the dragonfly. Cut a thin strip of paper and fold it into a zigzag. Glue one end to the card and the other to the dragonfly.

11. Put glue inside the top and side edges of your card. Don't glue the bottom edge. Press the front onto the card and leave the glue to dry.

Fantasy castle card

When you open this card, several layers spring up. This is called a V-fold mechanism because you glue shapes onto a base in a V shape.

You will need: one piece of thick paper at each of these sizes: 30 x 20cm (12 x 8in), 18 x 18cm (7 x 7in), 28 x 10cm (11 x 4in) and 10 x 4cm (4 x 1½in); craft knife; glue; bright paper for decorating.

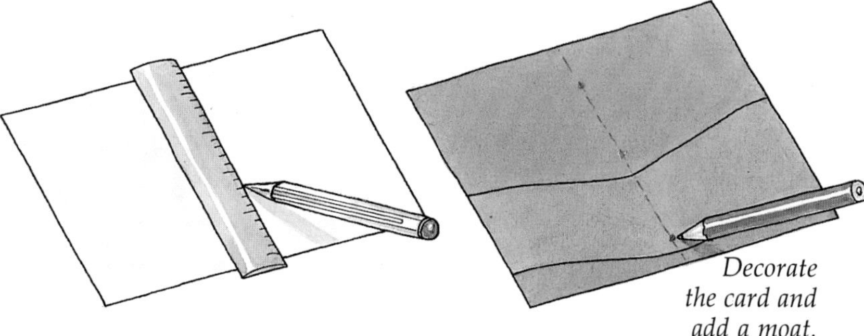

1. To make the base, make two marks halfway (15cm/6in) from one short end of the largest piece of paper. Score along the marks and fold it.

2. Cut a curved moat and glue it on near the bottom. Make marks on the fold 3.5cm (1½in), 9.5cm (3¾in) and 17cm (6¾in) from the top of the base.

3. Score a line (9cm/3½in) from one edge of the square piece of paper. Measure and score a line 1cm (½in) from the bottom edge.

4. Cut the bottom to make tabs. Draw a castle to fill the square, with its highest tower near the middle. Cut around the castle then fold it in half.

5. Bend the tabs back and glue the bottom of them. Line up the middle fold of the castle with the top mark on the base and press the tabs down.

6. Make marks halfway (14cm/5½in) along the long piece of paper. Score and fold along the marks. Also score a line 1cm (½in) from the bottom.

7. Draw some castle walls. Add a gateway, making the bottom of it touch the 1cm (½in) line. Cut out the castle, the gateway and some tabs.

8. Bend and glue the tabs. Line up the middle fold with the middle mark on the base. Press the tabs on at the same angle as those on the castle.

9. For a drawbridge, cut a strip of paper which is wider than your gateway and long enough to go over the moat. Score a tab at one end and glue it on.

This is the smallest piece of paper in the list of things you will need.

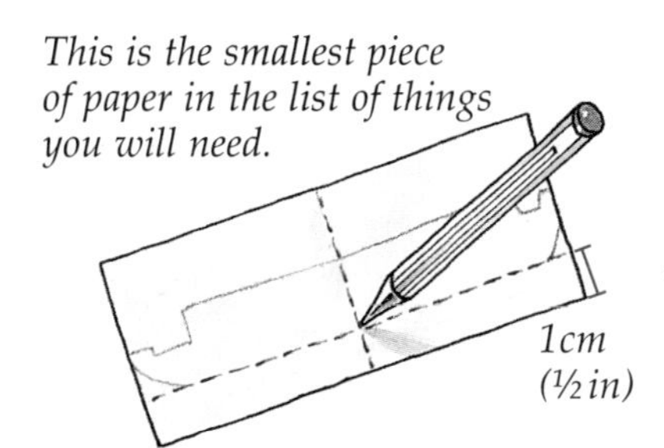

10. For the boat, score a line 5cm (2in) from one end of your paper. Score another line 1cm (½in) from the bottom and draw a boat along it.

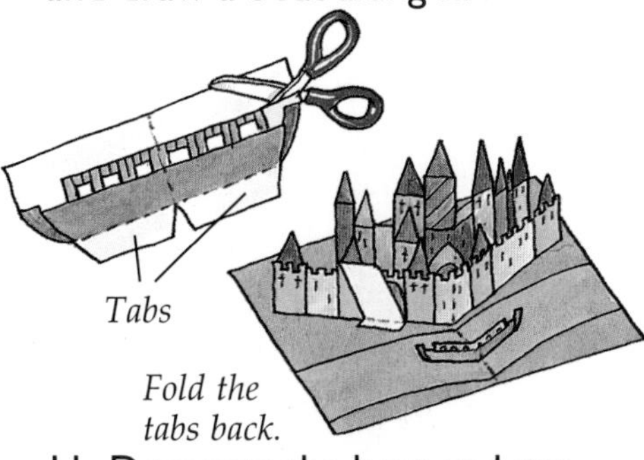

Fold the tabs back.

11. Decorate the boat and cut it out. Cut some tabs. Glue them then press the boat onto the base, lining up the middle fold with the bottom mark.

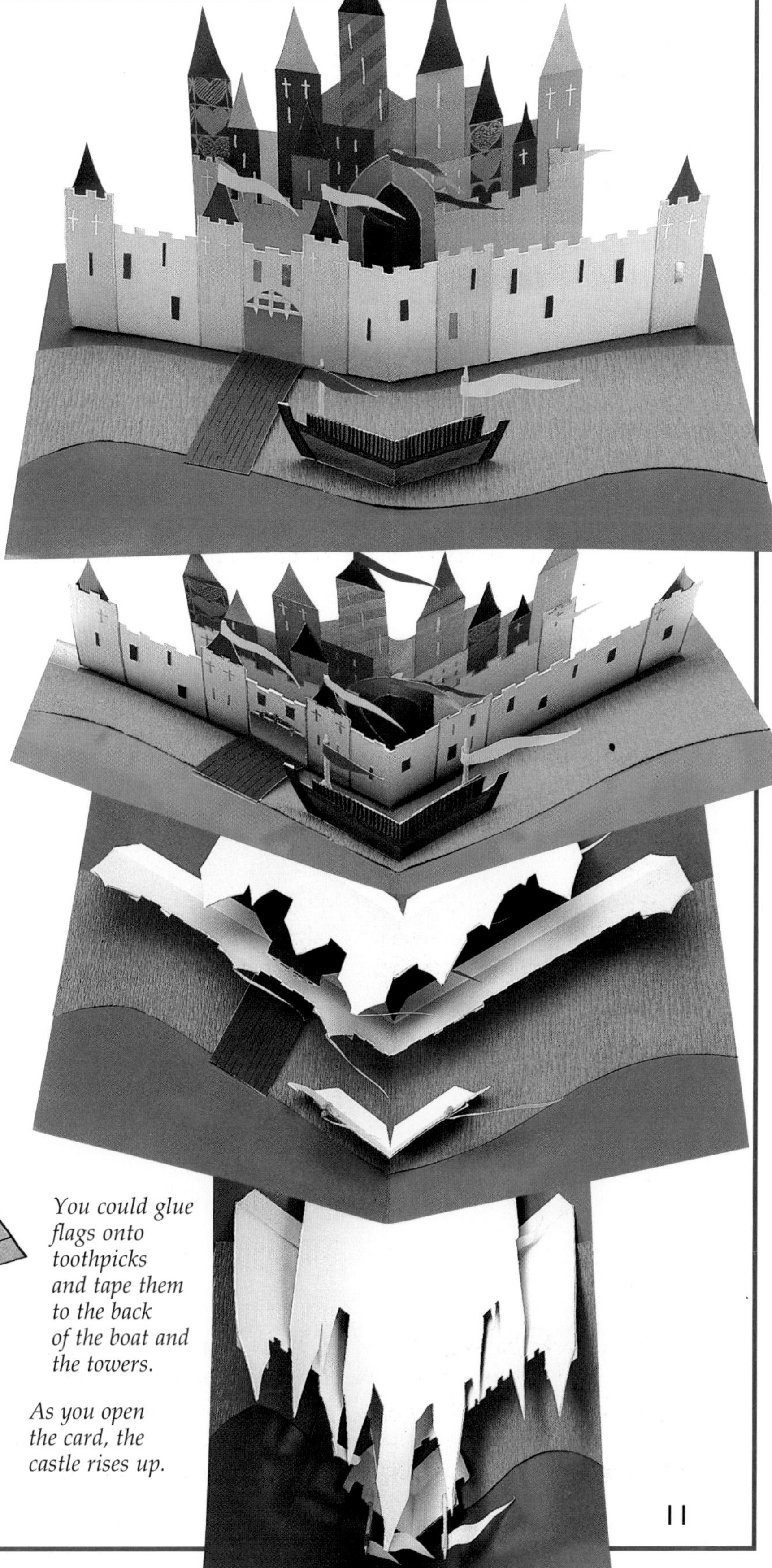

You could glue flags onto toothpicks and tape them to the back of the boat and the towers.

As you open the card, the castle rises up.

3-D card

This card folds completely flat, but when you open it, you'll be surprised at the layers inside.

You will need: thick paper 30 x 16cm (12 x 6¼in), 15 x 12cm (6 x 4¾in), 10 x 8cm (4 x 3¼in) and 4 x 3cm (1½ x 1in); gift wrap 30 x 16cm (12 x 6¼in); craft knife; glue; pens and paper for decorating.

1. For the background, glue the gift wrap to the biggest piece of paper. Make a mark halfway along each long side. Score between the marks.

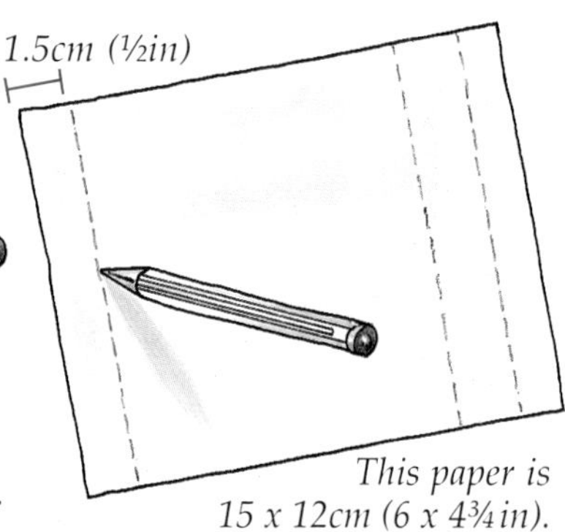

2. Make marks 1.5cm (½in) from the left end, and 1cm (⅜in) and 2.5cm (1in) from the right end of the paper. Score along each set of marks.

3. Draw a badger in its bed, but don't draw in the end sections. Cut it out. Trim the corners off the end sections at the top of the bed.

4. Fold the background in half and fold the bed along all its scored lines. Glue the left end section. Press it on the left side of the card, next to the fold.

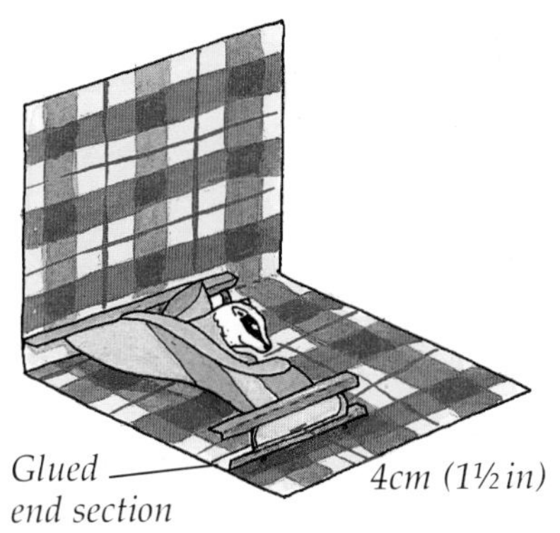

5. Mark 4cm (1½in) from the right edge of the card. Glue the end section of the bed and press it on, lining up the end of the bed with the marks.

6. On the second smallest piece of paper, mark and score lines at each end as you did in step 2. Draw a table in the sections shown above.

7. Cut around the outline of the table. Fold the left end section back then glue it. Press it onto the left side of the card, touching the bed.

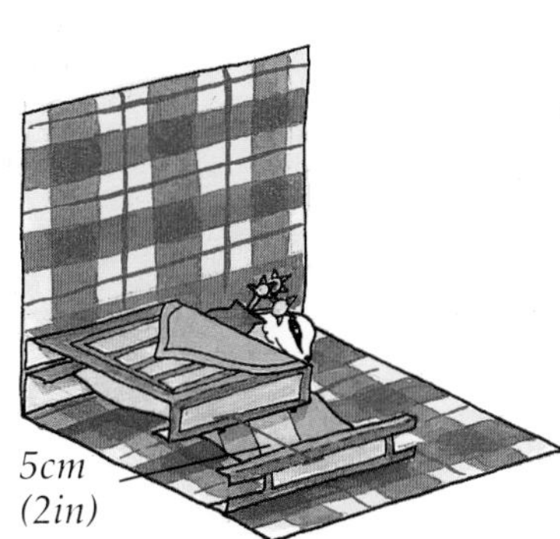

8. Make marks 5cm (2in) from the end of the bed. Glue the right end section and press it on, lining up the end of the table with the marks.

9. Draw a painting on the last piece of paper. Cut a strip of paper and fold it in half. Glue one side to your painting and the other side above the bed.

Other ideas

You can use this technique to make all kinds of different fold-away scenes.

To make a beach scene like the one below, draw the sky and sand on the background at step 1, a windbreak and umbrellas on the paper at step 3 and a bucket and beach ball at step 6.

For a city scene, fill the paper with skyscrapers at step 3 and draw a big yellow taxi and road at step 6.

To make these cards, see 'Other ideas'.

Twisting box heads

These heads are really upside-down boxes which you twist at the neck to open. The pattern may look a little difficult to draw, but it's easy if you measure the lines carefully.

You will need: very thick paper 25 x 20cm (10 x 8in); craft knife; felt-tip pens; glue; self-adhesive shapes and very thin wire for decorating.

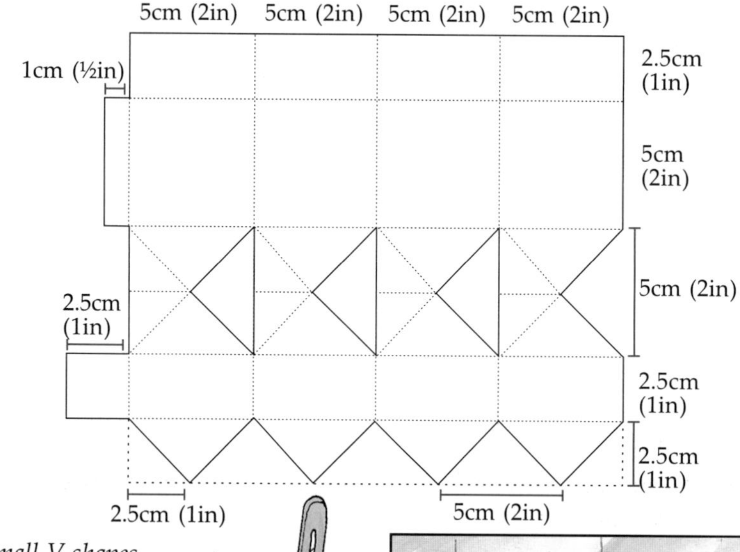

Cut the points.

1. Measure and draw the shape of the box onto thick paper. If you draw in the blue dotted lines it will help you to measure the points.

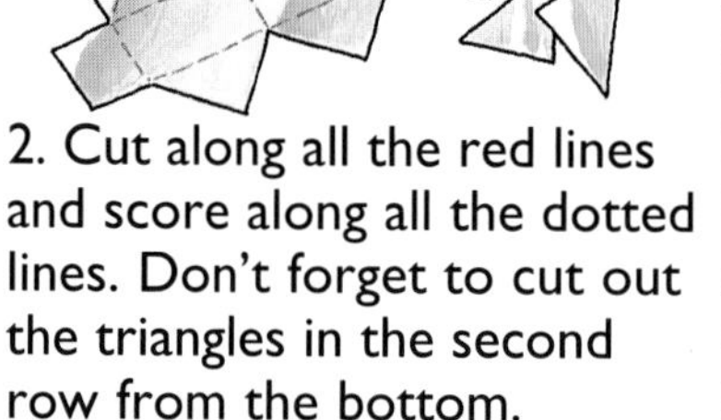

2. Cut along all the red lines and score along all the dotted lines. Don't forget to cut out the triangles in the second row from the bottom.

3. Fold the scored line between each triangle upward. At the same time fold the diagonal lines downward. Crease the lines well.

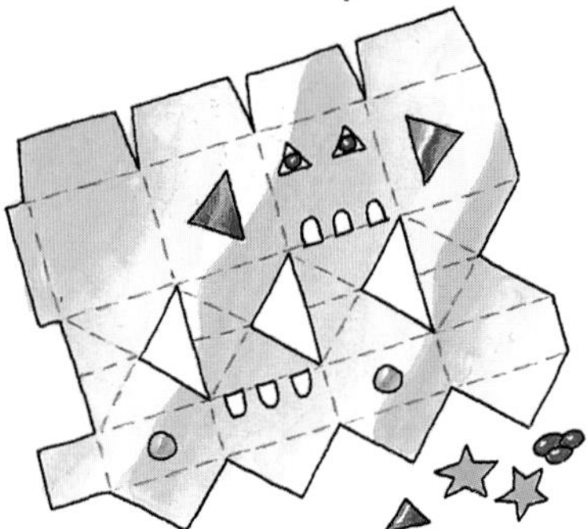

4. Lay your paper with the points at the bottom. Draw a face on the second square from the right, as above. Glue on shapes for decoration.

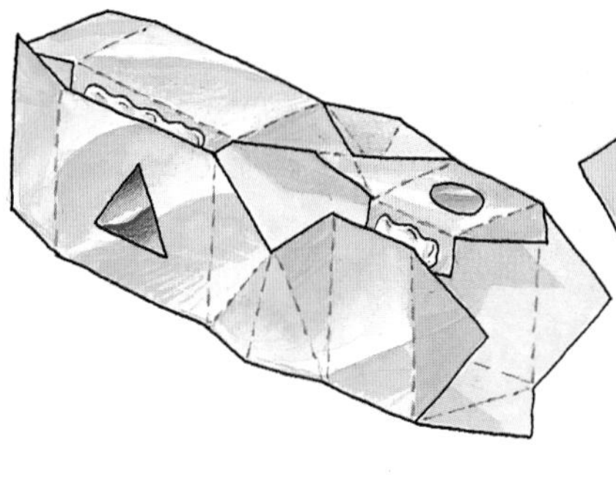

5. Fold all the scored lines. Glue the tabs at the side and fold the box around, lining up the edges as shown. Hold the tabs until the glue has dried.

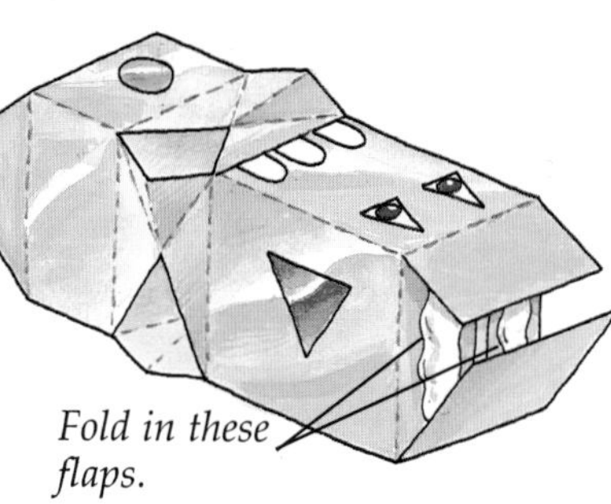

6. Turn the model like this and fold in two of the rectangular flaps. Put glue on them and press the other two flaps onto the glue.

7. Glue inside all the triangular flaps and fold them inward. Press them onto the sides of the box. This makes a firm base for your box.

8. Hold the box like this and press the ends together. Gently twist your right hand away from you then press the ends together again.

9. Cut two pieces of wire. Coil them around a pencil. Push them into the head. Untwist the box, bend ends of the wire and tape them.

Bus stop card

You will need: thick paper 30 x 18cm (12 x 7in) and two pieces of pale paper 16 x 25cm (7 x 10in); craft knife; scissors; glue; old ballpoint pen; scraps of thin paper for decorating; clear tape.

Measure and cut out this shape for A and B.

1. Make marks halfway (15cm/6in) along the large piece of paper. Score along the marks. Fold the paper in half then open it out again.

2. Draw a line 1.5cm (⅝in) to the left of the fold. Make marks from the bottom, as shown, then cut between them.

When you open this card, the movement pulls the two flat people into curved shapes.

Use thin paper to decorate the people so that the shapes can bend.

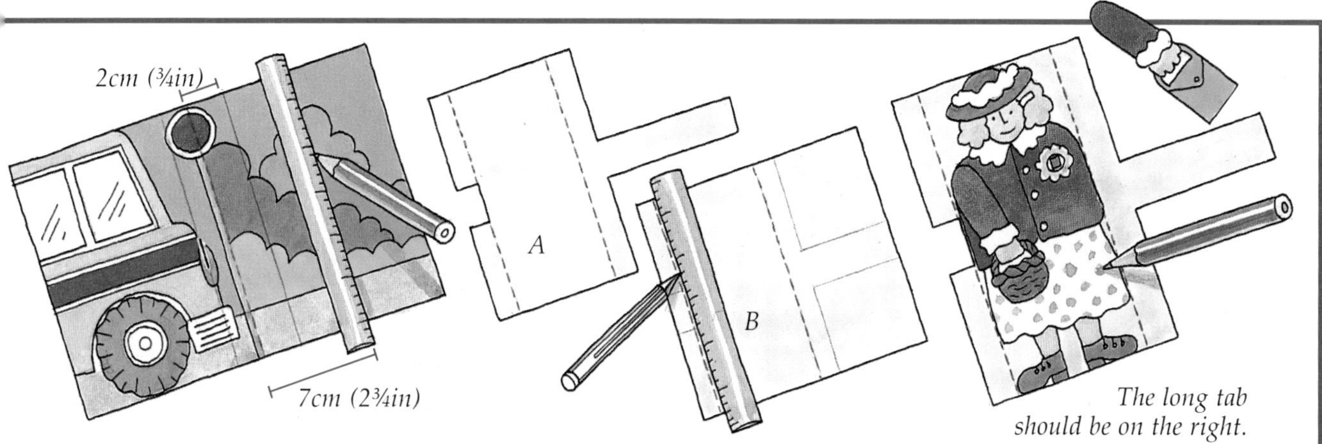

3. Draw or glue on a bus and a bus stop. Draw two lines on the right-hand side of the fold, one 2cm (¾in) from it, the other 7cm (2¾in) from it.

4. Measure and draw the shape for A and B (see left) onto pale paper. Measure and mark the dotted lines then score along them.

5. Draw a big person between the scored lines on both A and B. Draw or glue on bright clothes. Cut out arms from scrap paper and glue them on.

6. Fold along the scored lines to make tabs. Glue the two short tabs on the left side of A along the first pencil line on the right-hand side of the card.

7. Glue the short side tabs on B and press them onto the card, lining up their scored edge with the second pencil line. Leave the glue to dry.

8. Flatten B. Bend its long tab under and feed it through the gap between its short tabs. Then, feed B's tab through the gap between the tabs on A.

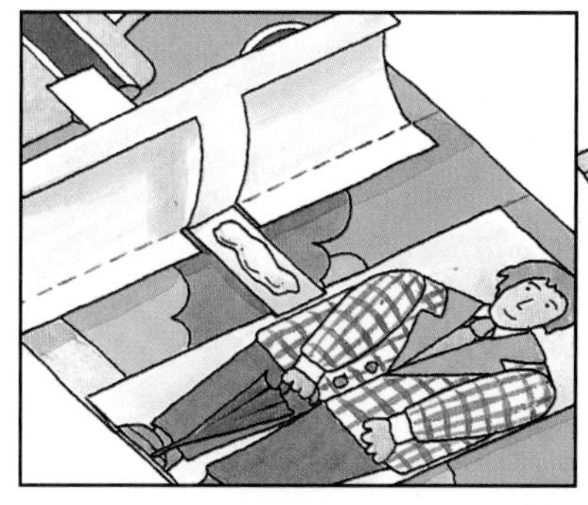

9. Bend A over and feed its long tab through the gap between its short tabs. Put a little glue on B's tab as shown and flatten A down onto it.

10. Lift up A's long tab and cut off the bottom tab close to the edge of A. Then feed A's long tab through the slot in left side of the card.

11. Close the card, pulling the tab through as far as it will go. Tape the tab to the front of the card then snip off the spare piece at the end of it.

Surprise box

When you open the lid of this box, a bug rises up and spreads its wings.

You will need: very thin cardboard 32 x 30cm (12½ x 12in) for the box, 12 x 12.5cm (5 x 5½in) for the top of the lid, 12 x 15cm (5x 6in) for the ends of the lid; craft knife; pair of compasses; scissors; glue.

If you want a different shade of paper inside, use two pieces of paper, glued together.

To make the box like this, glue on lentils and string. Cover them with gold paint when the glue is dry.

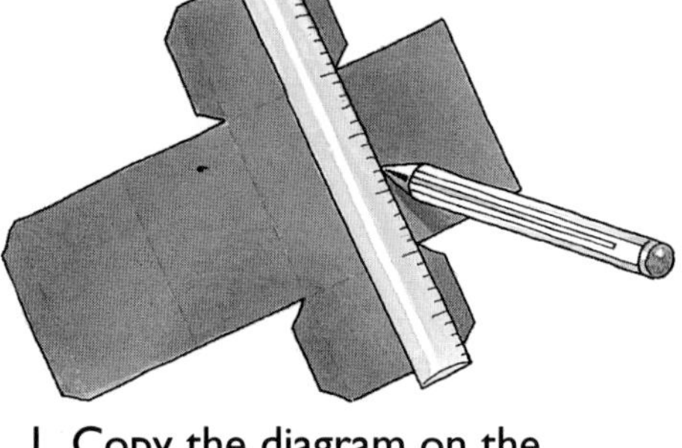

1. Copy the diagram on the left onto the large piece of cardboard. Score along the dotted lines. Cut it out and fold it along your scored lines.

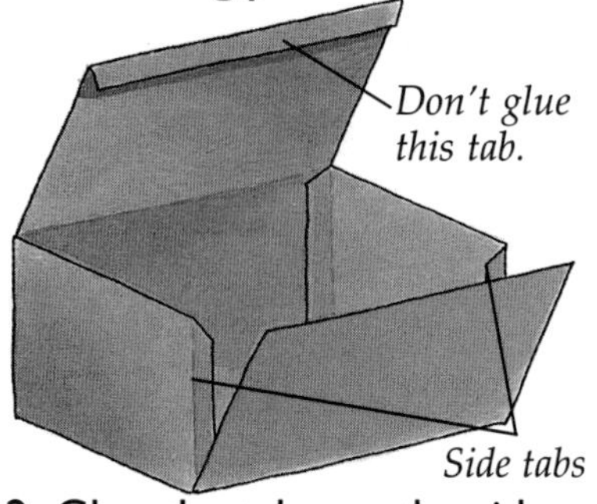

2. Glue the tabs on the side rectangles. Fold up the front and back of the box and press them onto the tabs. Make sure that all the edges line up.

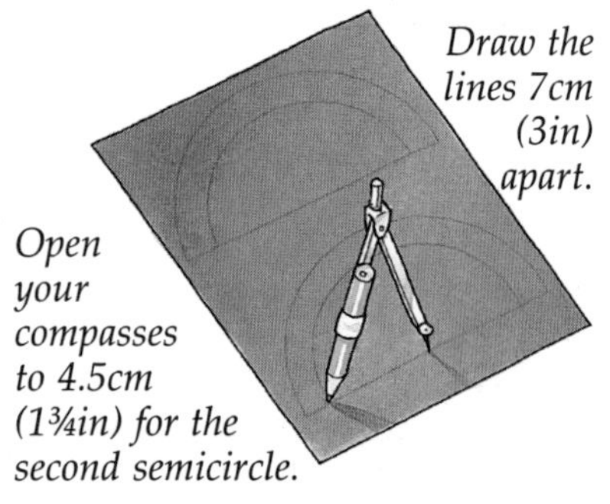

3. For the ends of the lid, draw two lines. Open your compasses to 3.5cm (1½in) and draw a semicircle on each line. Draw a second one around the edge.

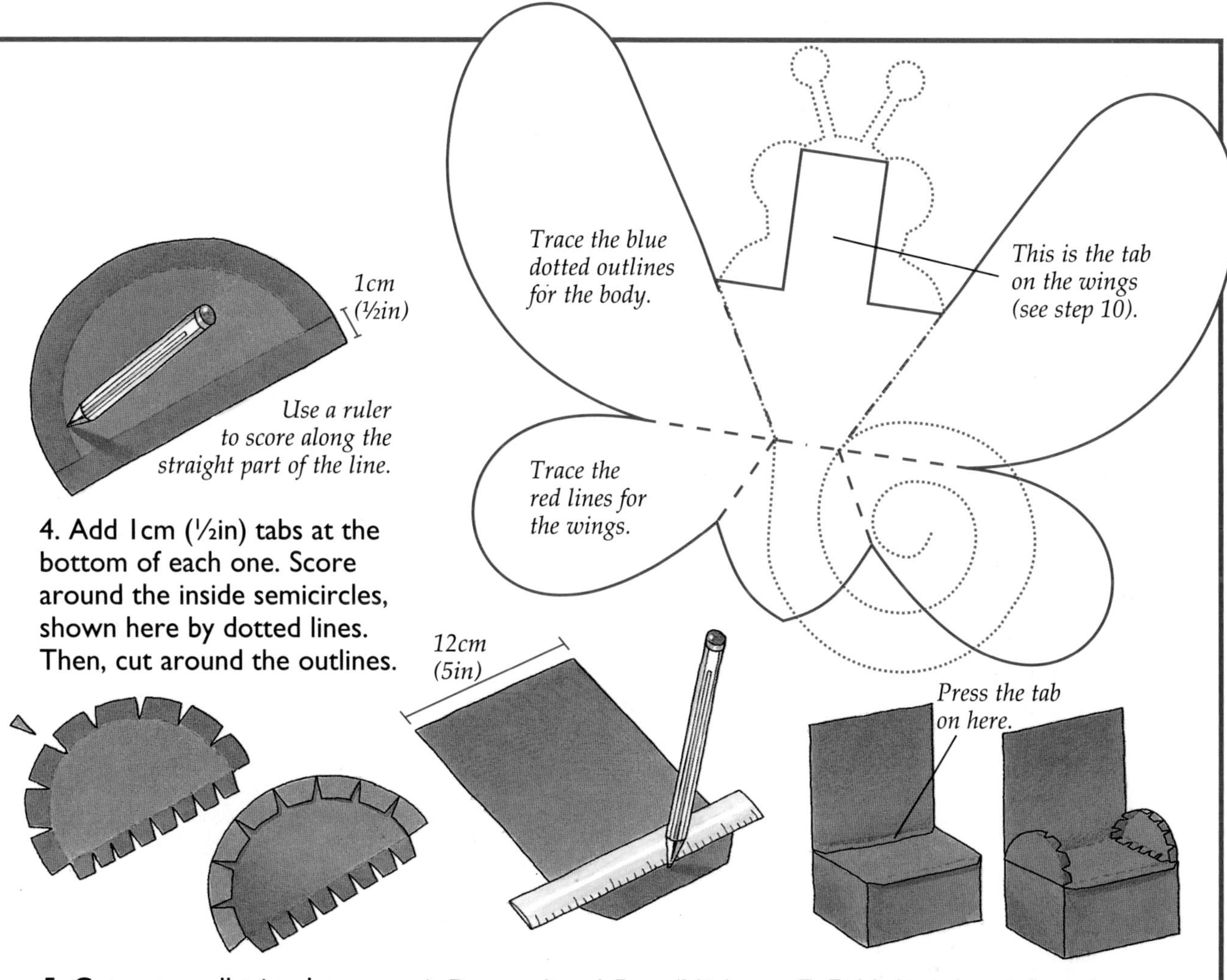

4. Add 1cm (½in) tabs at the bottom of each one. Score around the inside semicircles, shown here by dotted lines. Then, cut around the outlines.

5. Cut out small triangles around the edge, cutting in as far as the scored lines. Bend up the little tabs which are left around the semicircles.

6. Draw a line 1.5cm (¾in) from one end of the cardboard for the top of the lid and score along it. Cut off the corners to make a tab.

7. Fold the tab you have just cut and glue it on, as shown. Fold and glue the tabs on the bottom of the semicircles. Press one on at each end.

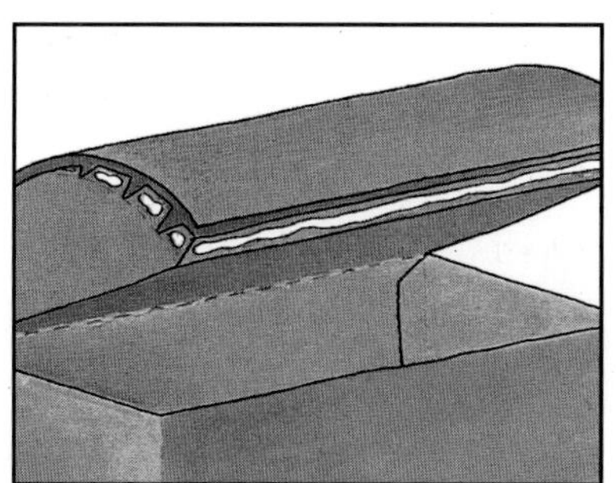

8. Fold up the tab at the front of the box. Glue this tab and all the little tabs. Before the glue dries, bend the top over and press it on the tabs.

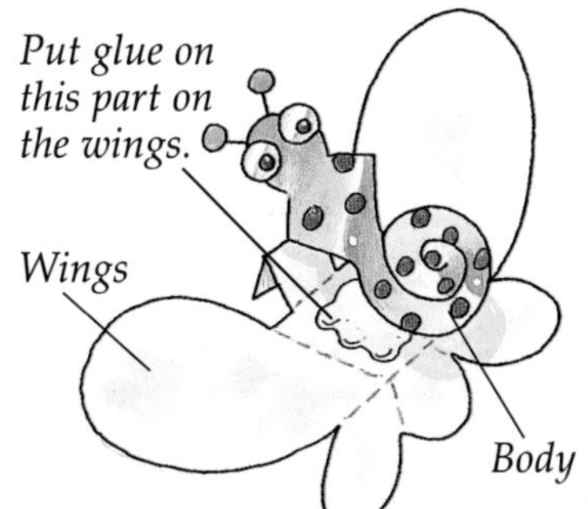

9. Trace the templates above for the bug and wings and cut them out. Score and fold the dotted lines. Put glue on the wings and press the body on.

10. Glue the tab on the wings and press it on the lid, above the 'hinge'. Glue the tip of the tail, stretch it a little and press it on the back of the box.

Marching elephants

If you move a hidden tab under the elephant's tummy, its head, tail and rider look as if the elephant is marching. You'll find all the templates you need on page 36.

You will need: a piece of thick paper 21 x 30cm (8½ x 12in); craft knife; glue; a split-pin paper fastener; toothpick; scraps of bright paper, threads and sequins for decorating.

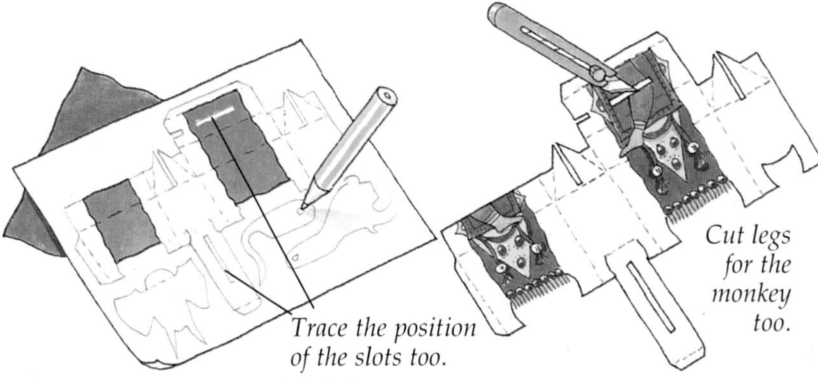

Trace the position of the slots too.

Cut legs for the monkey too.

1. Trace the templates of the body, head and tail templates onto paper. Trace the elephant's blankets too. Score along all the dotted lines.

2. Cut out all the shapes. Glue the blanket shapes onto the body piece, like this, lining up the scored lines. Cut the slot through both layers.

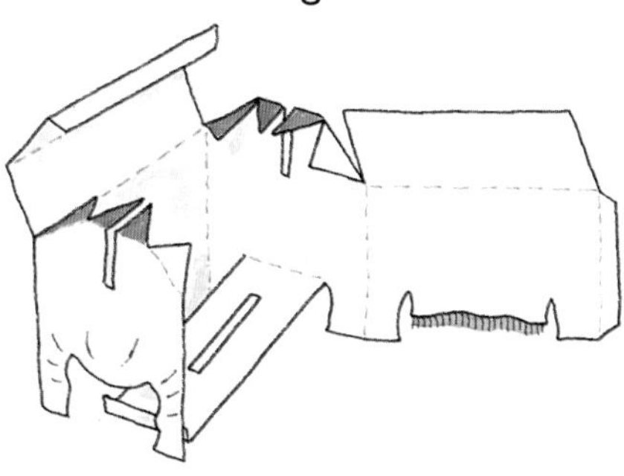

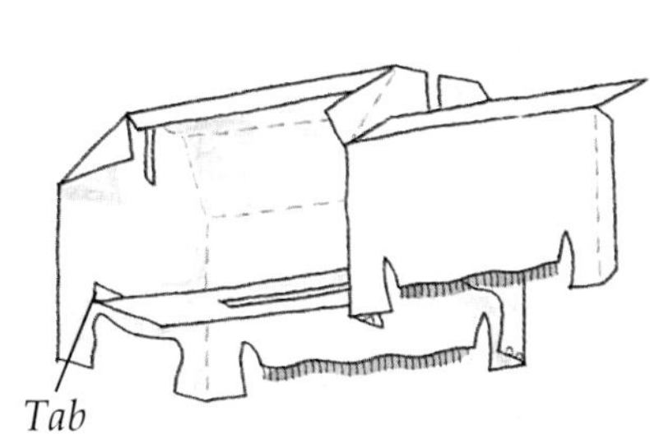

Tab

Make the umbrella any shape you like.

3. Glue all the triangular tabs shown here in red. Fold the body shape around and press the top of the elephant's body onto the tabs.

4. Fold the underneath section of the body upward and glue the tab. Press it on inside the body shape, between the elephant's back legs.

5. Trace, cut out and decorate the monkey. Cut out an umbrella and tape a toothpick to the back of it. Glue it onto the monkey's hand.

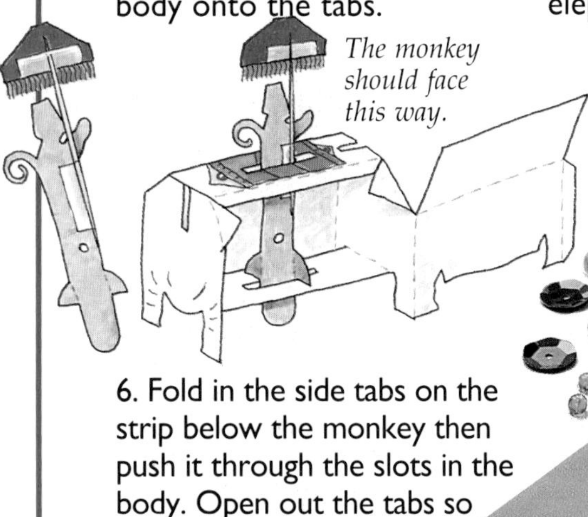

The monkey should face this way.

Use little pieces of embroidery thread, sequins and a gold pen to decorate your pieces.

6. Fold in the side tabs on the strip below the monkey then push it through the slots in the body. Open out the tabs so that they look like this.

Open the ends of the fastener to secure the pieces.

Leg tab

7. Slip the tail and neck into the slots in the body. Line up their holes with the one on the monkey. Push in a paper fastener and open its ends.

8. Glue the tabs on top and on the leg of the elephant. Fold the side onto the tabs and press the back part of the leg onto the leg tab.

Move the tab below the elephant's tummy up and down in a circle to make it look as if it is marching.

9. Decorate the head and fold along the scored lines. Fold and glue the tabs on the neck then press the middle of the head onto the tabs.

Once you have made your elephant, use a black felt-tip pen to draw wrinkles on its knees and trunk. Add toenails too.

Squawking parrot

When you turn the yellow handle on the base, the parrot's wings flap up and down and its beak opens and closes.

You will need: one piece of very thin cardboard 42 x 30cm (16 x 12in) for the body and wings, and one piece 21 x 30cm (8 x 12in) for the base; a piece of thin cardboard and a piece of corrugated cardboard 6 x 6cm (2½ x 2½in) for the circles; a drinking straw; a pin; a toothpick; poster mounting putty; a wooden kebab stick; household glue (PVA); felt-tip pens and bright paper for decorating.

You can find all the templates for the parrot's body, wings and bottom beak at the back of this book, on pages 30 and 31.

Decorate your parrot with tissue paper before you glue it together.

Cut out leaves and glue them on the base after you have finished.

Turn this handle to make the parrot move.

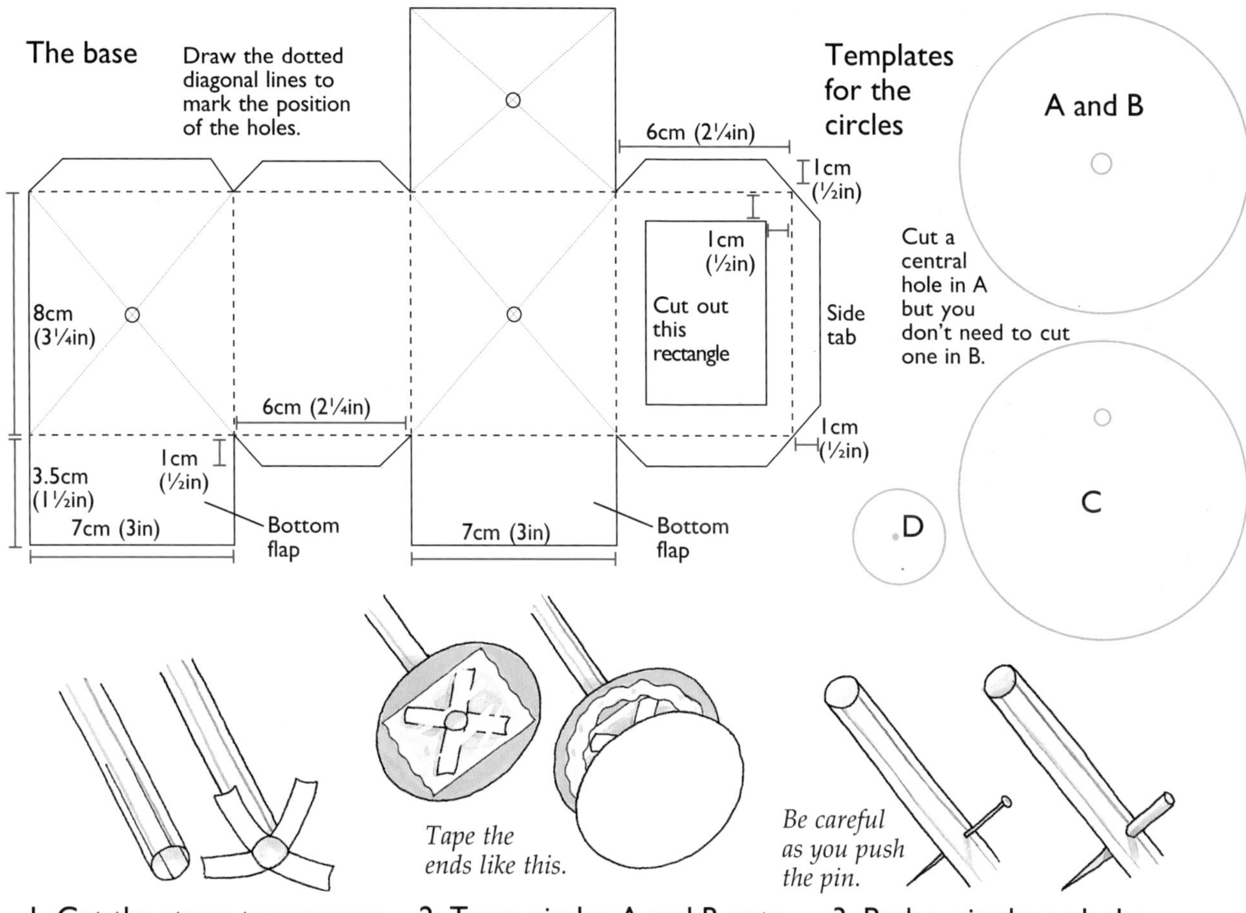

1. Cut the straw to measure 18cm (7in) then make four 1.5cm (½in) slits at one end. Bend the ends out to the sides to make this shape.

2. Trace circles A and B onto cardboard. Cut them out. Push the straw through the hole in A. Slide the circle down and tape it. Glue B over the tape.

3. Push a pin through the straw, 7.5cm (2¾in) from the top. Cut a piece of toothpick 5cm (2in) long and push it through the pinhole.

Poster putty

4. Make a sausage shape with some poster putty. Press it firmly onto the cardboard circle, around the bottom of the straw.

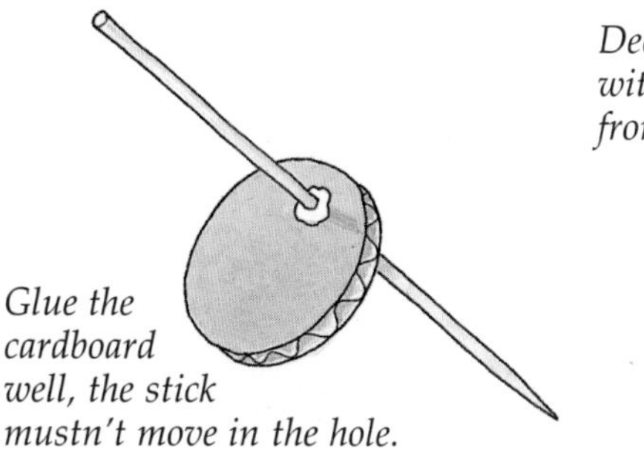

5. Trace circle C onto corrugated cardboard and cut it out. Cut the kebab stick to 9cm (3½in). Push it halfway through the hole and glue it.

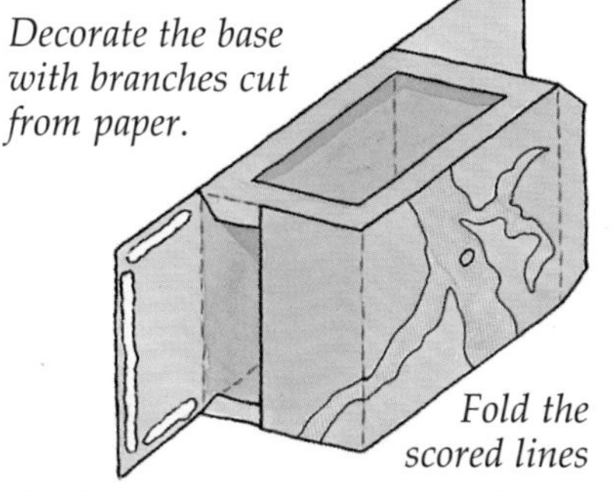

6. Draw and cut out the base. Glue the side tab and fold the sides around. Glue the bottom flaps and press them onto the bottom tabs.

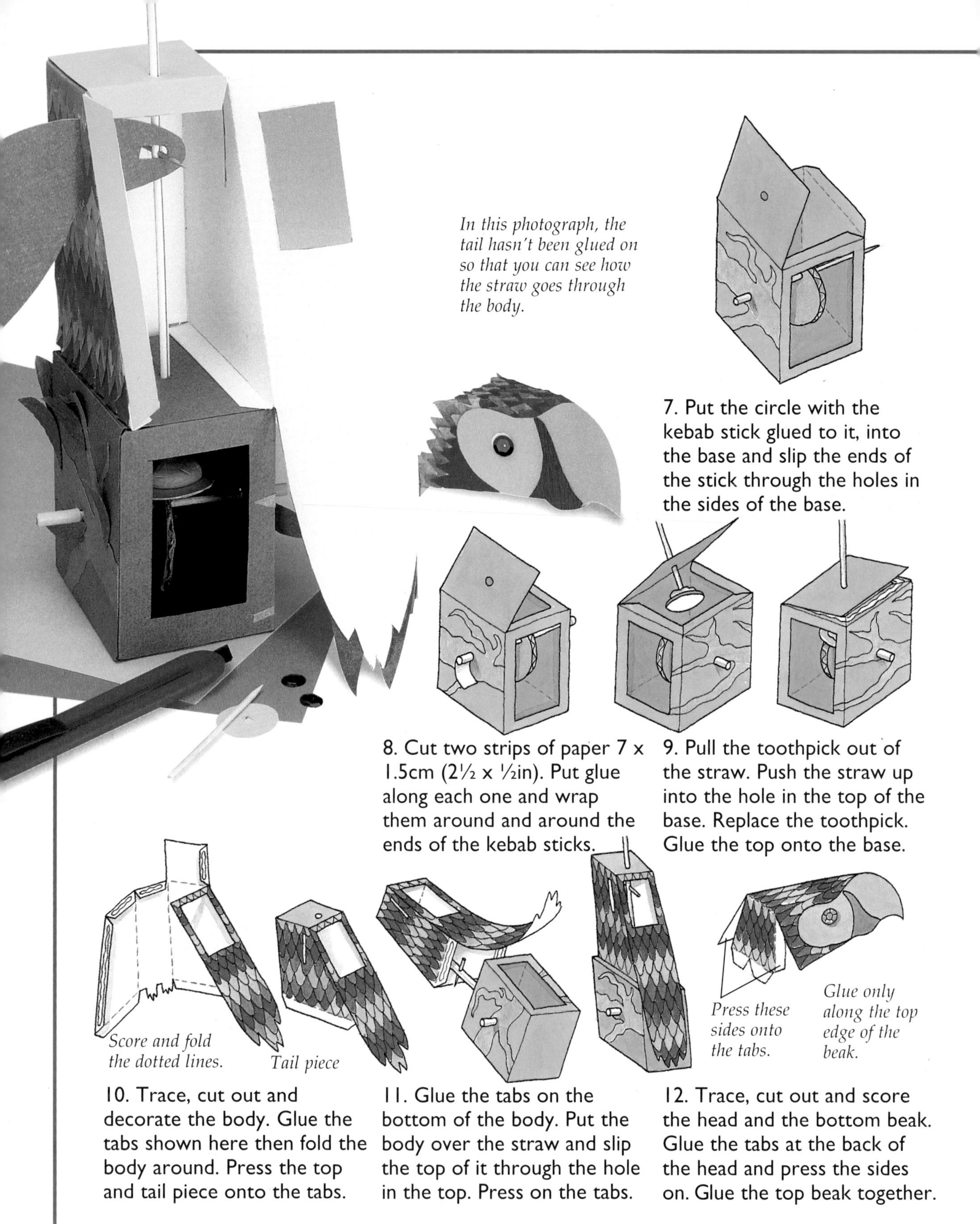

In this photograph, the tail hasn't been glued on so that you can see how the straw goes through the body.

7. Put the circle with the kebab stick glued to it, into the base and slip the ends of the stick through the holes in the sides of the base.

8. Cut two strips of paper 7 x 1.5cm (2½ x ½in). Put glue along each one and wrap them around and around the ends of the kebab sticks.

9. Pull the toothpick out of the straw. Push the straw up into the hole in the top of the base. Replace the toothpick. Glue the top onto the base.

10. Trace, cut out and decorate the body. Glue the tabs shown here then fold the body around. Press the top and tail piece onto the tabs.

11. Glue the tabs on the bottom of the body. Put the body over the straw and slip the top of it through the hole in the top. Press on the tabs.

12. Trace, cut out and score the head and the bottom beak. Glue the tabs at the back of the head and press the sides on. Glue the top beak together.

13. Glue the tab at the back of the head. Put the head over the straw and press the tab onto the body. Glue the bottom beak below the top one.

14. Trace, cut out and decorate two wings. Push them into the slots in the side of the body. Slip the slot in each wing onto the toothpick.

15. Trace and cut out circle D. Push a pin through the middle then slip it onto the toothpick, but not touching the wings. Add a little glue to secure it.

Other flapping birds

For these birds, follow the instructions for the squawking parrot, but use the templates for the wings and beaks on page 31.

Pirate ship

Turn to page 29 to see the spectacular pirate ship which lies completely flat when you close the background. All the templates for the pieces of the ship are on pages 32-24.

You will need: a piece of thick blue paper 60 x 40cm (24 x 16in); for the ship, one piece of paper 70 x 42cm (28 x 17in) or three pieces, paper 42 x 30cm (17 x 12in); craft knife; glue; scraps of paper.

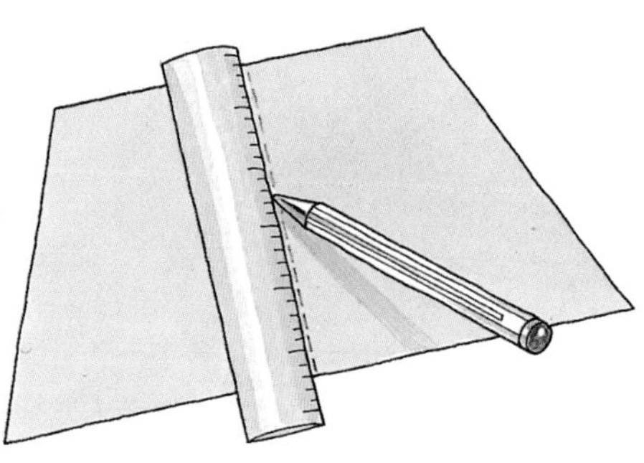

1. Make marks halfway (30cm/12in) along the long sides of piece of blue paper. Score a line along the marks and fold the paper in half.

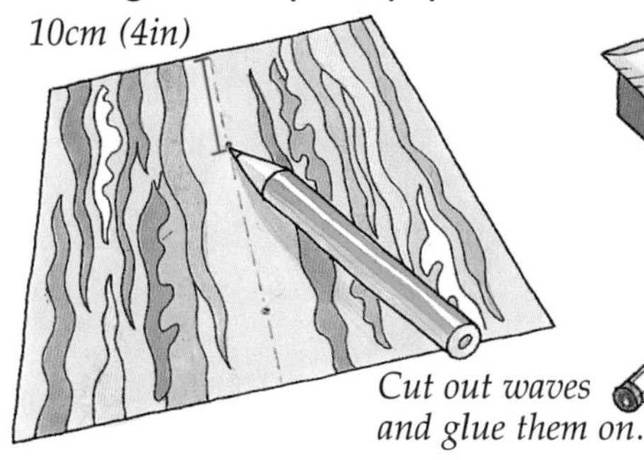

10cm (4in)

Cut out waves and glue them on.

2. Open out the paper and make a mark on the fold 10cm (4in) from the top. Measure another mark 8.5cm (3½in) from the bottom.

3. Trace template for the central support onto paper. Cut it out. Score along the dotted lines and fold along them for tabs.

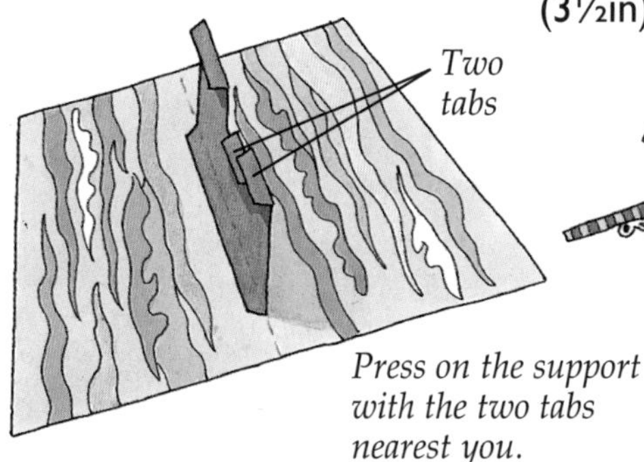

Two tabs

Press on the support with the two tabs nearest you.

4. Glue the long bottom tab. Line it up with the middle fold on the background and between the two marks you made in step 2. Press it on.

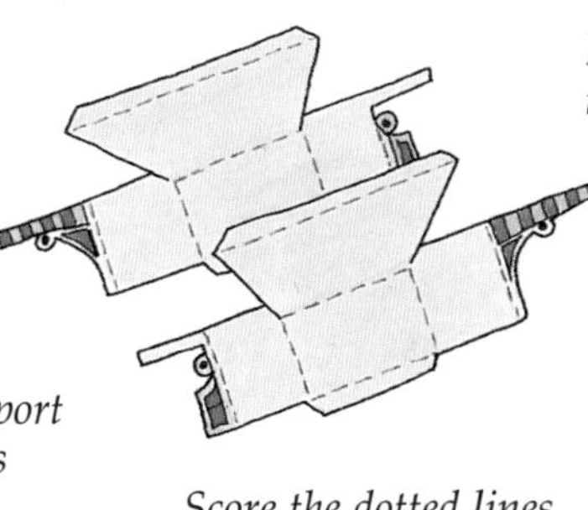

Score the dotted lines.

5. Trace the template for the ship's side twice. Cut out each piece then turn one of them over so that you have a left and a right side for your ship.

Draw planks on the deck.

Add port holes and cannons.

6. Decorate the sides. Cut out a wiggly strip of blue paper and glue it along the bottom of the ship, for waves. Fold along the scored lines.

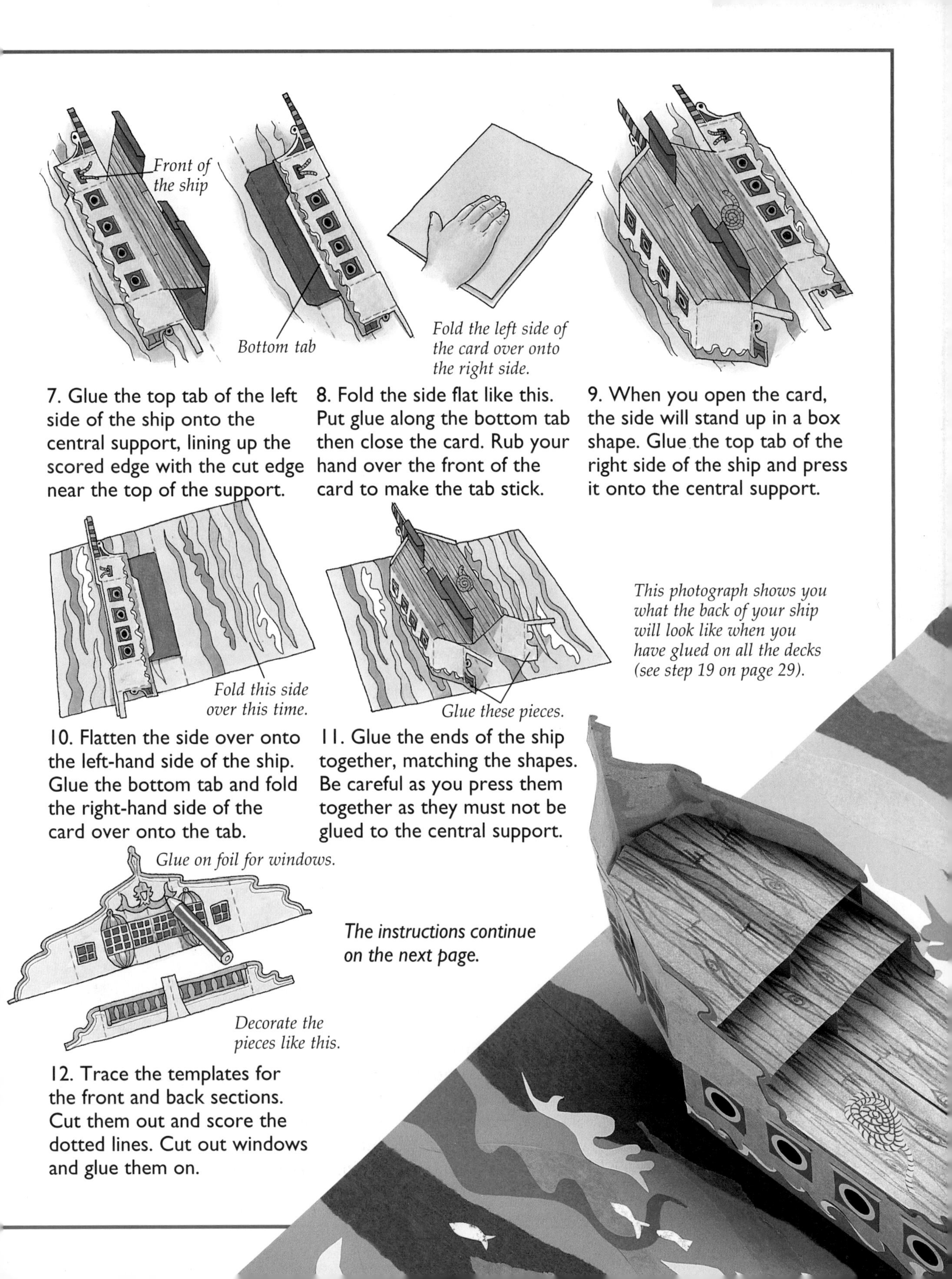

7. Glue the top tab of the left side of the ship onto the central support, lining up the scored edge with the cut edge near the top of the support.

8. Fold the side flat like this. Put glue along the bottom tab then close the card. Rub your hand over the front of the card to make the tab stick.

9. When you open the card, the side will stand up in a box shape. Glue the top tab of the right side of the ship and press it onto the central support.

This photograph shows you what the back of your ship will look like when you have glued on all the decks (see step 19 on page 29).

10. Flatten the side over onto the left-hand side of the ship. Glue the bottom tab and fold the right-hand side of the card over onto the tab.

11. Glue the ends of the ship together, matching the shapes. Be careful as you press them together as they must not be glued to the central support.

The instructions continue on the next page.

12. Trace the templates for the front and back sections. Cut them out and score the dotted lines. Cut out windows and glue them on.

Pirate ship continued

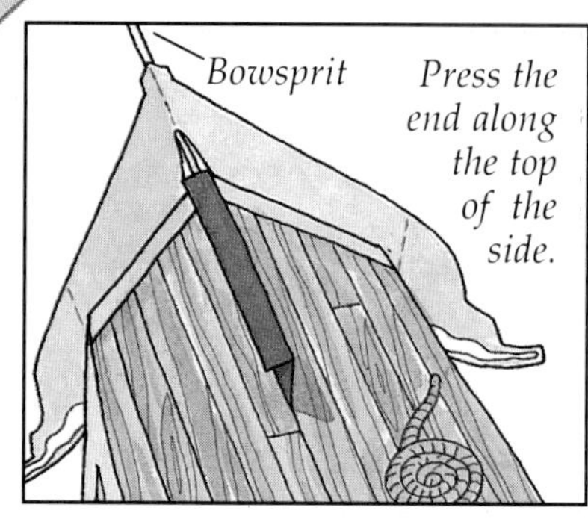

13. Glue the bottom of each end of the front section. Slip the notch over the bowsprit at the front of the ship and press each end onto the side.

Draw and cut out pirates like these. Add a tab beneath their feet and glue it onto the deck.

14. Glue along the bottom of each end of the back section. Press the ends onto the sides of the ship so that they line up with the edge of the deck.

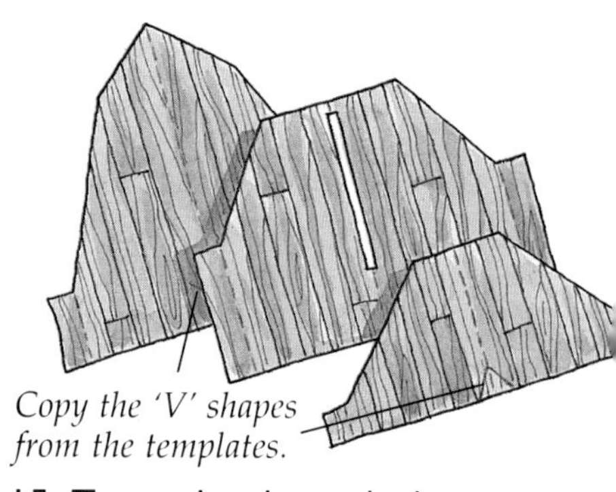

15. Trace the three deck pieces. Cut them out and score all their dotted lines. Use pens to decorate them with planks of wood.

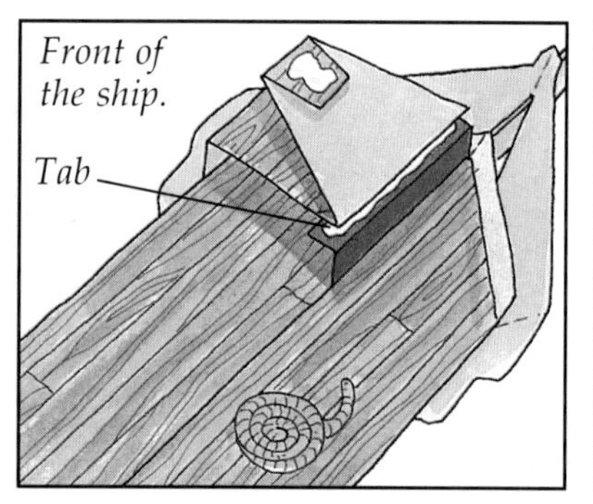

16. Fold the front top deck piece in half. Fold the single tab on the central support to the left and glue it. Press the left side of the deck onto it.

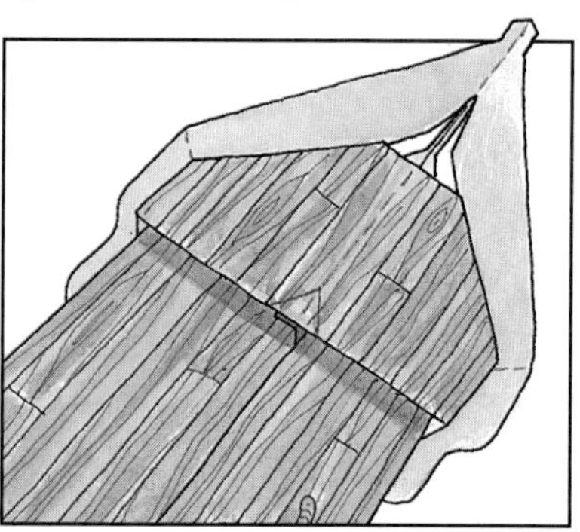

17. Open out the deck piece. Glue the top of the two small tabs, as shown in step 16. Press them onto the sides of the front section of the ship.

18. Slip the large tab of the central support through the slot in the middle deck. Glue the small tab and press the right side of the deck onto it.

19. Glue the side tabs of the middle deck to the sides of the ship. Glue the top deck onto the large tab and its small tabs onto the sides.

20. Trace, cut out and score the masts. Glue their tabs and press them onto the 'V' shapes on the decks. The tall one goes in the middle.

21. Trace the sails. Cut them out and decorate them. Glue the big sail onto the middle mast and the triangular sail on the front one.

Draw some flags and glue them on the top of the masts.

This pirate ship is 28cm (11in) tall, but lies completely flat when you close the card.

If you glue pirates onto the decks, make sure that they don't get in the way of the sails when you close the card.

Templates

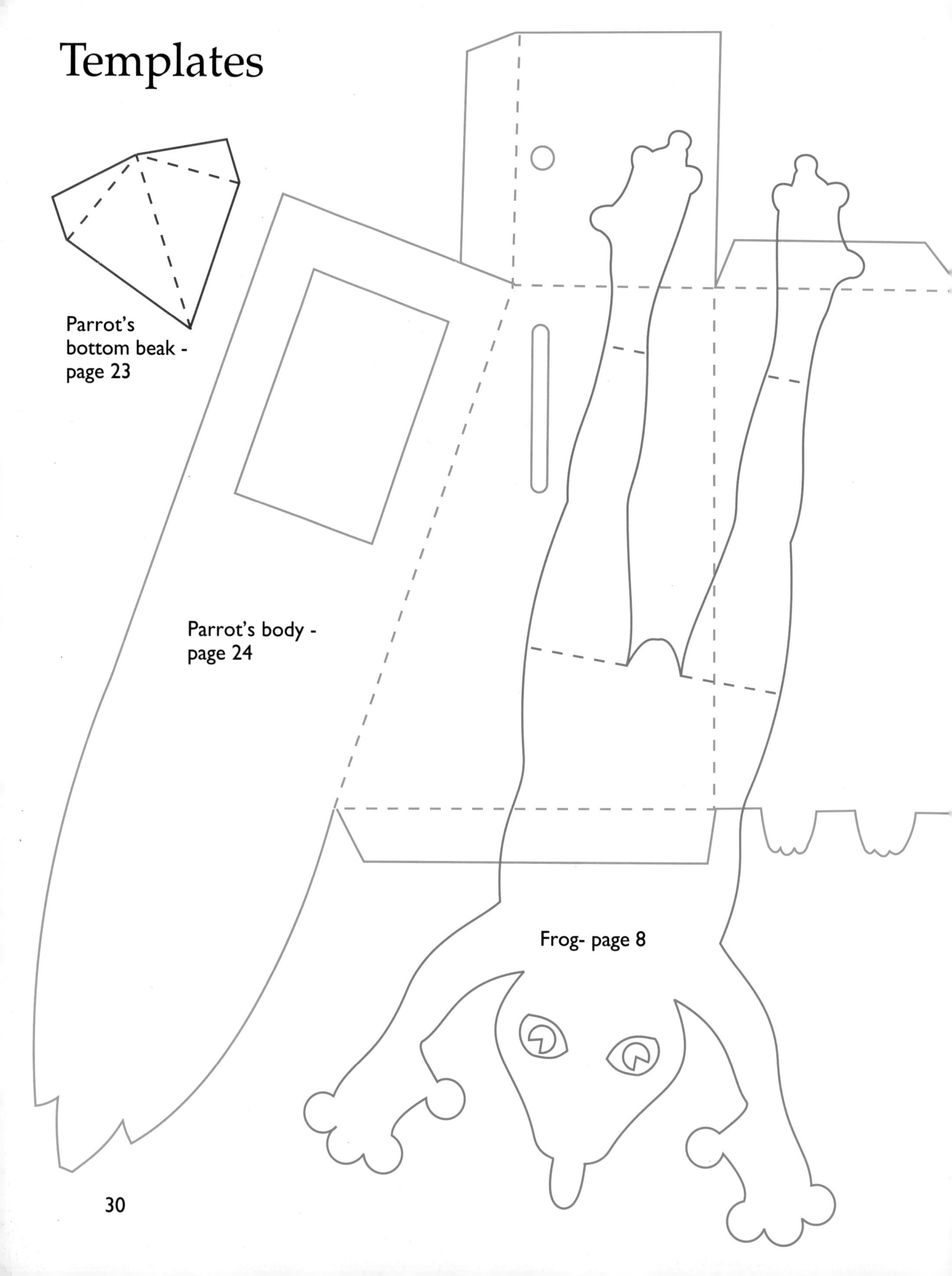

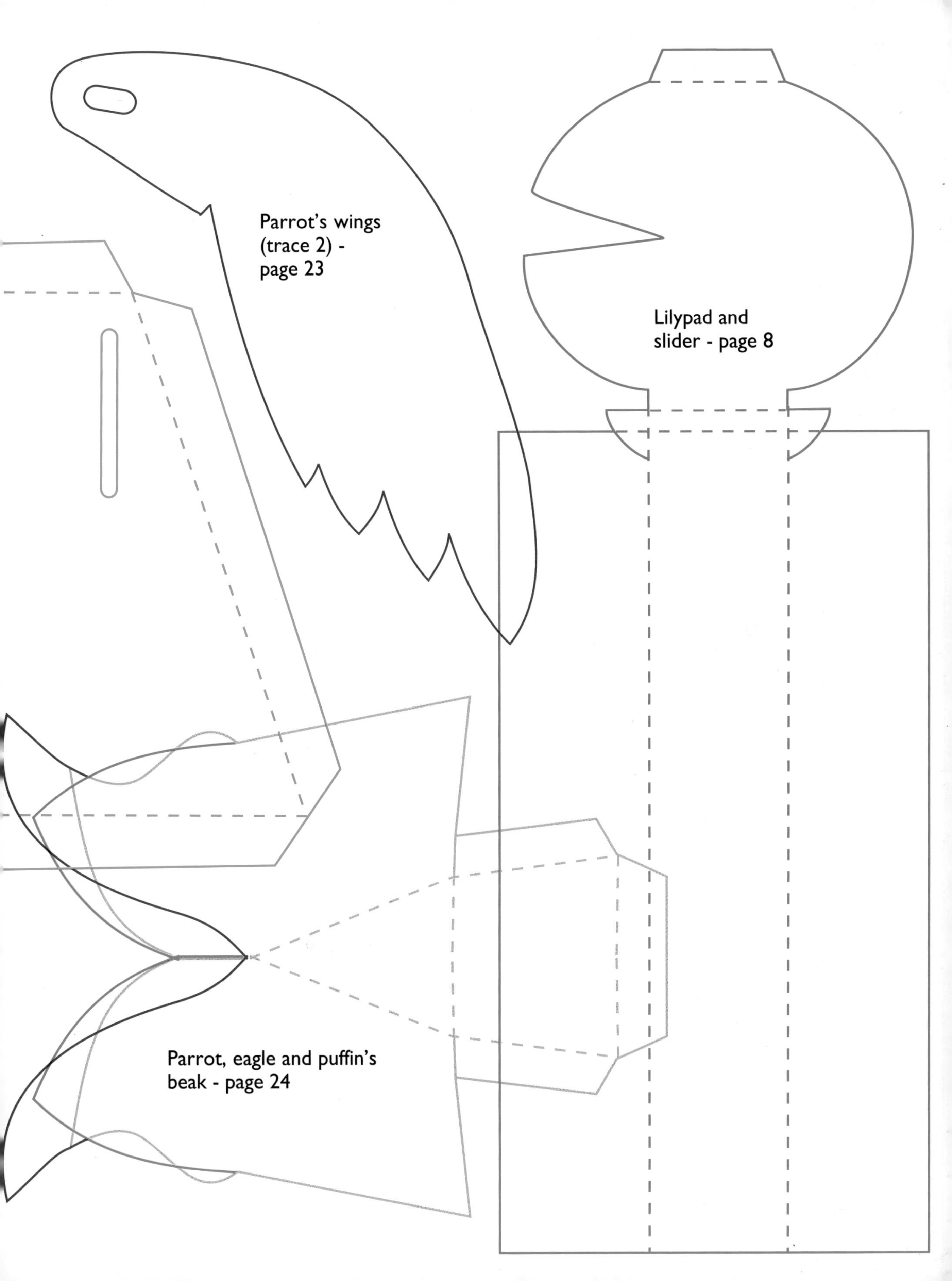
Parrot's wings
(trace 2) -
page 23
Lilypad and
slider - page 8
Parrot, eagle and puffin's
beak - page 24

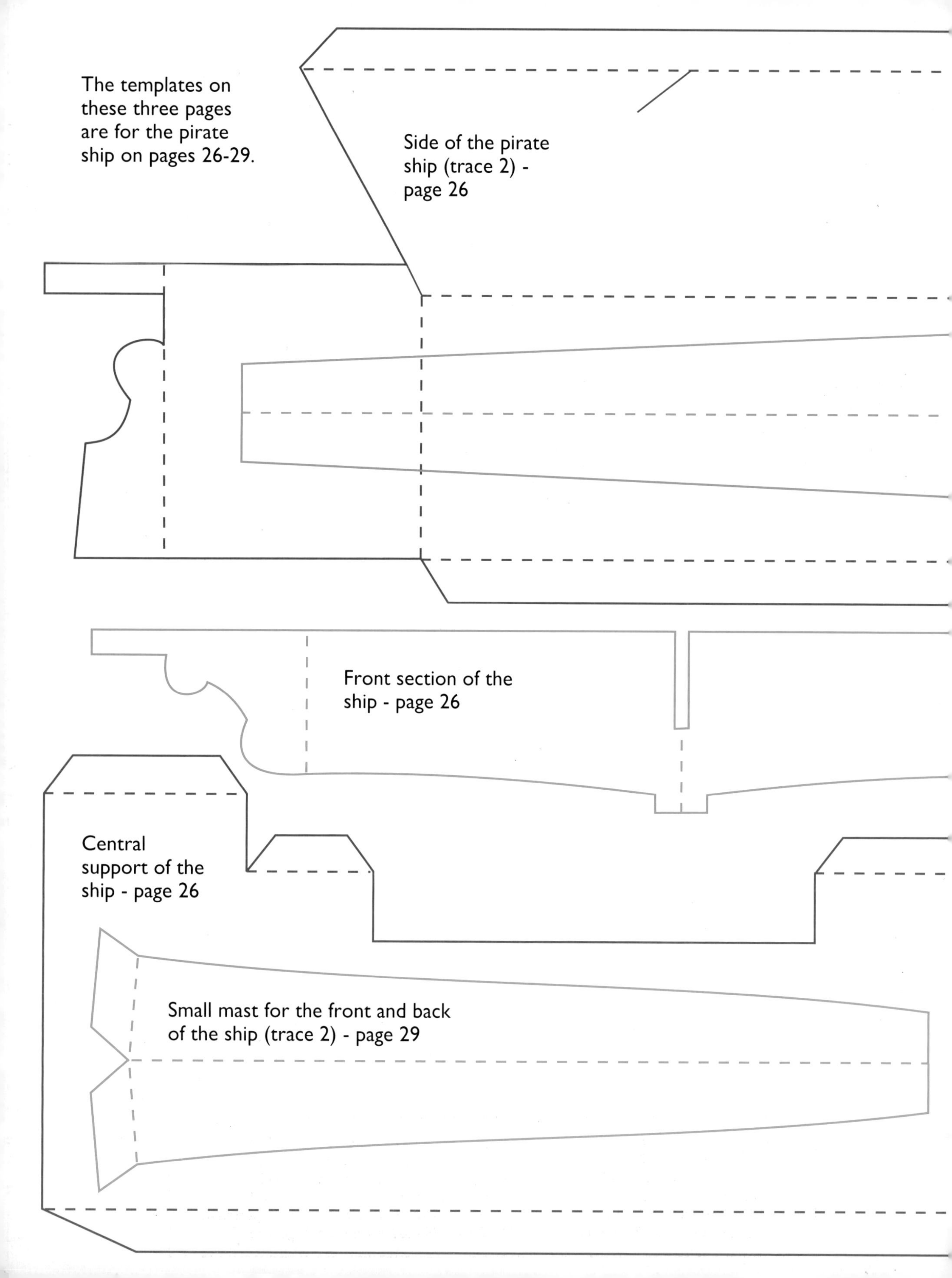
The templates on
these three pages
are for the pirate
ship on pages 26-29.
Side of the pirate
ship (trace 2) -
page 26
Front section of the
ship - page 26
Central
support of the
ship - page 26
Small mast for the front and back
of the ship (trace 2) - page 29